THE KILLING

The driver of the green car was saying something to Joseph Joe about the trailer, when a Ford sedan stopped just in front of the driver's car. A man wearing a plaid coat got out of it and walked toward them and then stopped suddenly, apparently noticing Joseph for the first time, and said, "We've got business, old man. You go away now."

Hosteen Joe had turned then and walked back toward his daughter's truck. Behind him he heard the sound of a car door opening. Then closing. A yell. The sharp clap of a pistol shot. And then another shot, and another, and another. When he turned he saw Plaid Coat on the gravel and the driver holding himself up by clinging to the door of his car. Then the driver got in and drove away.

People were running out of the Wash-O-Mat by then, yelling questions. But Hosteen Joe just looked at the Plaid Coat sprawled on his side on the gravel and got into his daughter's truck.

The driver was Navajo, but this was white man's business. . . .

Books by *Tony Hillerman*

FICTION

Sacred Clowns
Coyote Waits
Talking God
A Thief of Time
Skinwalkers
The Ghostway
The Dark Wind
People of Darkness
Listening Woman
Dance Hall of the Dead
The Fly on the Wall
The Blessing Way
The Boy Who Made Dragonfly
(for children)

NONFICTION

The Great Taos Bank Robbery
Rio Grande
New Mexico
The Spell of New Mexico
Indian Country

TONY HILLERMAN

THE GHOSTWAY

HarperPaperbacks
A Division of HarperCollinsPublishers

This is a work of fiction. The characters, incidents, and dialogues are products of the author's imagination and are not to be construed as real. Any resemblance to actual events or persons, living or dead, is entirely coincidental.

HarperPaperbacks *A Division of* HarperCollins*Publishers*
10 East 53rd Street, New York, N.Y. 10022

A hardcover edition of this book was published in 1984 by Harper & Row, Publishers, Inc.

Cover illustration by Peter Thorpe

First HarperPaperbacks printing: January 1992

Manufactured in the United Kingdom by HarperCollins*Publishers* Ltd.

HarperPaperbacks and colophon are trademarks of HarperCollins*Publishers*

10 9 8 7 6 5 4

For Margaret Mary

With special thanks to Sam Bingham and those students at Rock Point Community School who took time to help me understand how Navajos deal with the chindis of Dine' Bike'yah in 1984.

➤ 1 ◀

HOSTEEN JOSEPH JOE REMEMBERED it like this.

He'd noticed the green car just as he came out of the Shiprock Economy Wash-O-Mat. The red light of sundown reflected from its windshield. Above the line of yellow cottonwoods along the San Juan River the shape of Shiprock was blue-black and ragged against the glow. The car looked brand new and it was rolling slowly across the gravel, the driver leaning out the window just a little. The driver had yelled at Joseph Joe.

"Hey!" he'd yelled. "Come here a minute."

Joseph Joe remembered that very clearly. The driver looked like a Navajo, but yelling at him like that was not a Navajo thing to do because Joseph Joe was eighty-one years old, and the people around Shiprock and up in the Chuska Mountains called him Hosteen, which means "old man" and is a term of great respect.

Joseph Joe had put his laundry sack into the back of his daughter's pickup truck and walked over to the car. He noticed its plates weren't yellow, like New Mexico's, or white, like Arizona's. They were blue.

"I'm looking for a man named Gorman," the driver had said. "Leroy Gorman. A Navajo. Moved here little while ago."

"I don't know him," Joseph Joe had said. He had said it in Navajo, because when he got close he saw he had been right. The man was a Navajo. But the driver just frowned at him.

"You speak English?" the driver asked.

"I don't know Leroy Gorman." Hosteen Joe said it in English this time.

"He's been around here several weeks," the driver said. "Young fellow. Little older than me. Medium-sized. Hell, small as this place is, I'd think you'd have seen him."

"I don't know him," Joseph Joe repeated. "I don't live in this town. I live at my daughter's place. Out there near the Shiprock." Joseph Joe had gestured toward the Arizona border and the old volcano core outlined by the sunset. "Don't live in here with all these people," he explained.

"I'll bet you've seen him," the driver said. He took out his billfold and fished a photograph out of it. "This is him," the driver said and handed the photograph to Hosteen Joe.

Joseph Joe looked at it carefully, as courtesy demanded. It was a Polaroid photograph, like the ones his granddaughter took. There was something written on the back of it, and an address. The front was a picture of a man standing by the door of a house trailer, which was partly shaded by a cottonwood tree. Hosteen Joe took off his glasses and wiped them off carefully on his sleeve and looked a long time at the young man's face. He didn't recognize him, and that's what he said when he handed the driver his photograph. After that, he didn't remember the rest of it quite as clearly because just then it all began to happen.

The driver was saying something to him about the trailer, maybe about Gorman living in it or trying to sell it or something, and then there was the sound of a car braking on the highway, tires squealing a little, and the car backing up and whipping around and driving into the Wash-O-Mat parking lot. This car was new too. A Ford sedan.

It stopped just in front of the driver's car. A man wearing a plaid coat got out of it and walked toward them and then stopped suddenly, apparently noticing Joseph Joe for the first time. Plaid Coat said something to the driver. As Joseph Joe remembered, it was "Hello, Albert," but the driver didn't say anything. Then Plaid Coat said, "You forgot to do what you were told. You've got to come along with me. You're not supposed to be here." Or something like that. And then he had looked at Joseph Joe and said, "We've got business, old man. You go away now."

Hosteen Joe had turned then and walked back toward his daughter's truck. Behind him he heard the sound of a car door opening. Then closing. A yell. The sharp clap of a pistol shot. And then another shot, and another, and another. When he turned he saw Plaid Coat on the gravel and the driver holding himself up by clinging to the door of his car. Then the driver got in and drove away. When the car got to the asphalt, it turned toward the river and toward the junction, which would either take it west toward Teec Nos Pos or south toward Gallup.

People were running out of the Wash-O-Mat by then, yelling questions. But Hosteen Joe just looked at Plaid Coat, sprawled on his side on the gravel with a pistol on the ground beside him and blood running out his mouth. Then he got into his daughter's truck.

The driver was Navajo, but this was white man's business.

> 2 <

"FUNNY HOW A PREMONITION WORKS," the deputy said. "I been in this business almost thirty years, and I never had one before."

Jim Chee said nothing. He was trying to recreate precisely and exactly the moment when he had known everything was going wrong with Mary Landon. He didn't want to think about the deputy's premonitions. He'd said something to Mary about his house trailer being too small for both of them, and she'd said, "Hey, wait a minute, Jim Chee, what have you done about that application with the FBI?" and he'd told her that he'd decided not to mail it. And Mary had just sat there in the Crownpoint Café, not looking at him or saying anything, and finally she'd sighed and shook her head and said, "Why should you be any different from everybody else?" and laughed a laugh with absolutely no humor in it. He was remembering all this and concentrating on his driving, following the rocky track which led along this high hump of the Chuska Mountains. The moon was down and the night was in that period of implacable cold darkness that comes just before the first gray light of dawn. Chee was driving with only his parking lights—just as Sharkey had told him to drive. That meant going slowly and risking a wrong turn at any of the places where the trail divided itself to go wandering off toward a spring, or someone's hogan, or a sheep dip, or who knows what. Chee wasn't worried about the slowness. Sharkey's plan was to get to the hogan of Hosteen Begay long enough before daylight to let them get into position. There was plenty of time. But he was worried about a wrong turn. And his mind was full of Mary Landon. Besides, the deputy had said it all before.

Now the deputy was saying it all again.

"Had a funny feeling from the very first," the deputy said. "When Sharkey was telling us about it back there in Captain Largo's office. Felt the skin tightening on the back of my neck. Kind of a coldness. And prickling on the arms. Somebody's going to get hurt, I thought. Somebody's going to get their butt shot off."

Chee sensed the deputy was looking at him, waiting for him to say something. "Um," Chee said.

"Yes," the deputy agreed. "I got a feeling that Gorman fella's laying up there with his pistol cocked, and when we walk in somebody's going to get killed."

Chee eased the Navajo Tribal Police carryall around a washout. In his rearview mirror he could see the parking lights of Sharkey's pickup truck. The FBI agent was staying about a hundred yards behind him. The deputy now interrupted his monologue to light a cigaret. In the flare of the kitchen match, the man's face looked yellow—an old and sinister face. The deputy's name was Bales and he was old enough, with even more years weathered into his skin by the high-country sun of San Juan County. But not sinister. His reputation was for easygoing, over-talkative mildness. Now he exhaled smoke.

"It's not a feeling that I'm going to get shot," Bales said. "It's a sort of general feeling that somebody will."

Chee was conscious again that Bales was waiting for him to say something. This white man's custom of expecting a listener to do more than listen was contrary to Chee's courteous Navajo conditioning. He'd first become aware of it his freshman year at the University of New Mexico. He'd dated a girl in his sociology class and she'd accused him of not listening to her, and it had taken two or three misunderstandings before

he'd finally fathomed that while his people pre-
sume that if they're talking, you are listening,
white people require periodic reassurance. Deputy Sheriff Bales was requiring such reassurance now, and Chee tried to think of something
to say.

"Somebody already got shot," he said. "Couple of people got shot, including Gorman."

"I meant somebody new," Bales said.

"If it's not you," Chee said, "that leaves me, or
Sharkey, or that other FBI agent he brought
along. Or maybe Old Man Begay."

"I don't think so," Bales said. "I think it would
need to be one of us, the way this premonition
feels." Satisfied now that Chee was listening,
Bales inhaled deeply and allowed a moment of
silence while he savored the taste of the tobacco.

Mary Landon had stirred her coffee, looking
at it and not at him. "You've made up your mind
to stay," she'd said. "Haven't you. When were
you going to tell me?" And he'd said what? Something stupid or insensitive, probably. He
couldn't remember exactly what he'd said. But
he remembered her words—vividly, clearly, exactly.

"Whatever you say about it, it just has one
meaning. It means I come second. What comes
first is Jim Chee, being Navajo. I'm to be sort of
an appendage to his life. Mrs. Chee and the

Navajo children." He'd interrupted her, denying that accusation, and she had said the Navajo Way was important to him only when it reinforced what he already wanted to do. She'd said that before, and he knew exactly what was coming. The Navajos, she'd reminded him, married into the wife's clan. The husband joined the wife's family. "How about that, Jim Chee?" she'd asked. There was nothing he could say to her.

The deputy exhaled again and rolled down the window a bit to let the cold air suck out the smoke. "Always chaps my butt the way the FBI won't ever tell you anything," he said. "The subject is Albert Gorman." Bales raised the pitch of his voice a notch in a weak attempt to mimic the West Texas sound of Agent Sharkey. " 'Gorman is believed armed with a thirty-eight-caliber pistol.' " Bales switched back to his own rusty voice. "Believed, hell. They took a thirty-eight slug out of the guy he shot." Bales switched voices again. " 'Los Angeles informs us that it is particularly important to apprehend this subject alive. He is wanted for questioning.' " Bales snorted. "Ever arrest anyone who wasn't wanted for questioning about something?" Bales chuckled. "Like how many beers he had before he started driving."

Chee grunted. He eased the carryall around a place where the soil was cut away from a ridge

of stone. The rearview mirror assured him
again that Sharkey's pickup was still behind
him.

"I don't see how we can compromise," Mary
Landon had said. "I just don't see how we can
work it out." And he'd said, "Sure, Mary. Sure
we can." But she was right. How could you compromise it? Either he stayed with the Navajo
Police or he took a job off the reservation. Either he stayed Navajo or he turned white. Either
they raised their children in Albuquerque, or
Albany, or some other white city as white children or they raised them on the Colorado Plateau as Dinee. Halfway was worse than either
way. Chee had seen enough of that among dis-
placed Navajos in the border towns to know.
There was no compromise solution.

"You know what we heard?" the deputy said.
"We heard that this business was tied up with an
FBI agent getting killed out in L.A. We heard
that Gorman and Lerner, the guy he shot at the
laundry, was both working for some outfit on
the Coast. Some outfit that stole cars. Big operation. And some big shots got indicted. And an
FBI agent got knocked off. And that's why the
Feds are so hot to talk to this Gorman."

"Um," Chee said. He steered the carryall cautiously around a juniper, but not cautiously
enough. The left front wheel dropped into a

hole the parking lights hadn't revealed. The jarring jolt shook the deputy's hat down over his eyes.

"The car the dead guy was driving," the deputy said. "It was rented there at the Farmington airport. They tell you that?"

"No," Chee said. As a matter of fact, they hadn't told him anything much—which was exactly what Chee had learned to expect when he was running errands for the Federals. "Got a little job for you," Captain Largo said. "We need to find that fellow in the parking lot." It had seemed an odd thing to say, since the Shiprock agency of the Navajo Tribal Police, along with every other cop along the Arizona-New Mexico border, had all been looking for that fellow. But Chee had also come to expect Largo to say odd things. Largo had then explained himself by handing Chee a folder. It included a copy of the photograph of Albert Gorman that the FBI had provided, a rap sheet showing several arrests and one conviction for larceny of motor vehicles, and some biographical statistics. There were no blank spaces on the forms used by the Los Angeles Police Department for the sort of information Chee needed: Gorman's mother's name and her clan, which Albert Gorman had been "born to," and the clan of Gorman's father, which Albert had been "born for." Unless Albert

Gorman had forgotten how to be a Navajo in Los Angeles or, as sometimes happened off the reservation, had never learned the Navajo Way, the homes of these clansmen would be the place to look for Albert Gorman. Largo knew that.

"What I want you to do is drop everything else you're fooling around with. Just come up with this guy," Largo had said. "He didn't pass the roadblocks at Teec Nos Pos, and we had a car there fifteen minutes after the shooting, so he didn't go west. And he didn't get to the road-block at Sheep Springs, so he didn't get through us going south. So unless he turned east to Burnham, and that road doesn't go anyplace, he must have gone up into the Chuskas."

Chee had agreed to that, mentally changing the "must have" into a "most likely."

Largo pushed himself out of his chair and walked to the wall map, a bulky man with a barrel chest and thin hips—the top-heavy wedge shape so common among western Navajos. He waved a finger around a portion of the map encompassing the Shiprock massif, the Carrizo and Lukachukai mountains, the north end of the Chuskas, and the country between them. "Narrows it down to this little area," Largo said. "See how quick you can find him."

The little area was about the size of Connecticut, but its population wouldn't be more than a few hundred. And the few hundred would be people who would unfailingly notice and remember anything unusual. If Gorman had driven his green sedan into the country south of Teec Nos Pos, or west of Littlewater, it would have been seen and talked about and remembered—the subject of speculation. It was simply a matter of driving and driving and driving, and talking and talking and talking, for however many days it took to track it down. "How quick I find him depends on how lucky I get," Chee said.

"Get lucky, then," Largo said. "And when you find him, just call in. Don't try to arrest him. Don't go anywhere near him. Don't do nothing to spook him. Just get on the radio and get word to us, and we tell the Agency." Largo was leaning against the map, staring at Chee, expression neutral at best. "Understand what I'm saying? Don't screw it up. It's an FBI case. It is not, repeat not, a case for the Navajo Tribal Police. It's an Agency case. It is not our affair. It is not the affair of Officer Jim Chee. Got it?"

"Sure," Chee said.

"Chee finds. Chee calls in. Chee leaves it at that. Chee does not do any freelance screwing around," Largo said.

"Right," Chee said.

"I mean it," Largo said. "I don't know much about it, but from what I hear, this guy is tied up somehow or other with some big case in Los Angeles. And an FBI agent got killed." Largo paused long enough to allow Chee to consider what that meant. "That means that when the FBI says they want to talk to this guy, they *really* want to talk to him. You just find him."

And so Chee had found him and now, having found him, was guiding in the FBI to finish the job, with Deputy Bales along to properly represent the San Juan County Sheriff's Department.

Deputy Bales stifled a yawn. "Yeah," he said. "The dead guy came in on a chartered plane. Or anyway, the people at the airport said a private plane flew in, and he got out of it and rented the car. A hood out of Los Angeles. With a long rap sheet."

"Um," Chee said. He'd heard about the plane and the rented car and the police record. The homicide was exotic enough to be fuel for gossip. The FBI told nobody anything. But the Farmington police told the New Mexico State Police, who told the Sheriff's Office, who told the Navajo cops, who told the Bureau of Indian Affairs law and order people, who told the Arizona Highway Patrol. In the small, dull world of law enforcement, anything unusual is a precious commodity, worth weeks of conversation.

"I wonder if he really is wounded," the deputy said.

"Pretty sure about that," Chee said. "Old Joseph Joe is supposed to have seen him hanging on the car door, looking hurt. And when I looked in the car, there was blood on the front seat."

"Been wondering about that," the deputy said. "How'd you find it?"

"Just took time," Chee said. "You know how it is. Just keep asking until you ask the right person."

It had taken three days to find the right person, a boy getting off the bus from the Toadlena school. He'd seen the green sedan going by on the road that led from Two Gray Hills southward toward Owl Springs. Chee had stopped at the Two Gray Hills Trading Post and got a fix on who lived down that road and how to find their places. Then another hard afternoon of driving on doubtful trails. "Found it about dark yesterday," he added.

Bales had tilted his hat far back on his head. "And Sharkey decides to wait and catch him about daylight, when he's sleeping. Or when we hope he's sleeping. Course we don't even know he's there."

"No," Chee said. But he had no doubt at all that Albert Gorman was there. This terrible road led to the Begay hogan and nowhere else. And from his abandoned car, Gorman's tracks led toward the Begay place. They were the uncertain, wavering tracks of a man either drunk or badly hurt. And finally, there was what he'd learned at the trading post at Two Gray Hills on his way back. The trader wasn't there, but the woman handling the cash register had told him that, yes, Old Man Begay had a visitor.

"Hosteen Begay came in three-four days ago and asked what medicine to buy for somebody who hurt himself and had a lot of pain," she'd said. She'd sold him a bottle of aspirin and a stamp for an envelope he'd wanted mailed.

For several hundred yards the dim parking lights had been picking up the black gloss of spilled crankcase oil. Now they reflected from a green Plymouth sedan, blocking the trail. Chee parked his truck behind it, cut the lights and the engine, and climbed out.

Sharkey had the window of his pickup down. He was leaning out, looking at Chee.

"About three quarters of a mile up the track here," Chee said, pointing.

It was then he noticed for the first time that fog was forming. A trace of it drifted like gray smoke through the beam of Sharkey's lights just as he turned them off, and then the smell of fog was in Chee's nostrils and the dampness on his face.

3

IN THE HIGH, DRY MOUNTAINS of the Colorado Plateau, fog is out of its element. It forms as part of a climatic accident, produced when a cold front crosses a mountain range and collides with warmer air on the opposite slope. And it survives no longer than a fish out of water. By dawn, when the four of them reached the place of Hosteen Begay, the fog had already lost its character as a solid blinding cloud. Now it survived only in pockets, as patches and fragments. Chee stood at the edge of one such fragment, exactly where Sharkey had told him to stand—on the slope west of the meadow where Begay had built his hogan. His role was to make sure that if Gorman tried to escape he would not escape in that direction. Chee rested a hip against a boulder. He waited and watched. At the moment, he watched Deputy Bales, who stood beside a ponderosa pine, right hand against the tree trunk and his left holding a long-barreled revolver, its muzzle pointing at the ground. The bottom of the tree trunk and Bales's lower legs were obscured by the mist, making—in the dim light—man and tree seem somehow detached from solid earth. Over the meadow, the fog was almost solid, frayed only here and there by the very beginning of a cold dawn breeze. Chee glanced at his watch. In eleven minutes it would be sunrise.

The hogan was a little below where Chee and the deputy waited. Through the ebbing mist, Chee could make out its conical roof, which seemed to be formed of slabs sliced from ponderosa logs in their first trip past the blade at the sawmill. The mist eddied and obscured this and eddied again. The short tin smoke pipe jutting from the center of the roof cone seemed to be blocked, closed by something pressed up into it from inside the hogan. Chee stared, straining his vision. He could think of just one reason to block a hogan's smoke hole.

Chee clicked his tongue, producing a nondescript sound just loud enough to catch the deputy's attention. Then he motioned his intention to move. Bales looked surprised. He tapped the face of his wristwatch, reminding Chee of the few minutes left. Just at sunrise, Sharkey and his man would be at the hogan's east-facing door. If Hosteen Begay emerged to bless the new day in the traditional fashion, they would pull him out of harm's way, rush into the hogan, and overpower Gorman. If he didn't appear, they'd rush in anyway. That was the plan. Chee had a feeling now that it would be an exercise in futility.

He moved along the slope away from Bales toward the north side of the hogan. From what Chee had learned of Hosteen Begay at Two Gray Hills he was an old-fashioned man, a traditional man, a man who knew the Navajo Way and followed it. He would have built this hogan as Changing Woman taught—with a single doorway facing the direction of dawn, the direction of all beginnings. North was the direction of darkness, the direction of evil. It was through the north wall of a hogan that a corpse must be removed in the sad event of death striking someone inside. Then the smoke hole would be plugged, the entrance boarded, and the place abandoned—with the corpse hole left open to warn the People that this had become a death hogan. The body could be removed, but never the malicious *chindi* of the dead person. The ghost infection was permanent.

Chee had circled about a hundred yards, keeping out of sight. Now he was almost due north of the place. Through the thinning mist he could see the dark hole where the logs of the wall had been chopped away. Someone had indeed died inside the hogan of Hosteen Begay and left his ghost behind.

> 4 <

"**T**HE THING TO DO IS FIND THE BODY—if there is one," Sharkey said. "You take care of that, Chee. We'll see what we can find around here."

Sharkey was standing at the hogan doorway, a small, hard-looking man of maybe forty-five with blond hair, short-cropped and curly.

"Here's some more old bandage." Bales's voice came from behind Sharkey, inside the hogan. "Dried blood on this one, too."

"What else are you finding?" Chee asked. "Any bedroll?"

"See if you can find where they put the body," Sharkey said, his voice impatient.

"Sure," Chee said. He already had an idea where the body might be. From the description they had of Gorman he wouldn't be particularly heavy. But Begay was an old man, and carrying a full-sized corpse wouldn't be easy. Probably he'd have dragged it on the blankets that had been its bed. And the best convenient burial site was obvious. A line of cliffs towered over Begay's little meadow to the northwest, their base littered with giant sandstone boulders tumbled out of their walls. It was the ideal place to put a body where it would be safe from predators. Chee headed for the talus slope.

Sharkey's agent was climbing out of the arroyo that ran behind the hogan. He nodded at Chee. "Nothing in the corral or the sheep pens," he said. "And the manure looks old."

Chee nodded back, wishing he could remember the man's name and wondering what "old" meant when he defined animal droppings. Yesterday or last year? But he wasn't particularly interested in any of this. It was Sharkey's business, and none of his own. Gorman might be a Navajo by blood but he was a white man by conditioning, by behavior. Let the whites bury the whites, or however that quotation went. He needed to get back to Shiprock, back to his own work and his own problems. What was he going to do about Mary Landon?

Chee followed the only relatively easy pathway into the boulders, noticing very quickly that he'd guessed right. Something heavy had been dragged here, leaving a trail of broken weeds and disturbed dust. Then Chee noticed, just up the talus slope ahead of him, the raw

scar where rocks had been dislodged—pried
and pushed to cause gravity to produce a rock-
slide. The easy way to cover a body. Then he saw
blue denim.

The body had been placed atop a slab of stone
that had tumbled out of the cliff eons earlier.
The corpse was out of reach of coyotes there,
and the stones pushed down atop it had made it
safe from birds. The denim that had caught
Chee's eye was the bottom of a trouser leg. He
walked around the burial, inspecting it. He
could see nothing of the head and little of the
body, just the sole of the right shoe and, through
a gap between stones, a bit of the shoulder of a
blue shirt.

Something was bothering Chee, something a
touch out of harmony with things as they
should be. What? He climbed the slope and inspected the burial site from above. Just an un-
natural-looking slide of rocks. He looked
beyond it, inspecting the place of Hosteen
Begay. The sun was up now, high enough above
the horizon to be warm on his face. Below, the
hogan was still in shadow. A neat place, well
made, with a well-made brush arbor beside it,
and a fairly new Montgomery Ward storage
shed, and a welded pipe rack for the oil drums
in which Hosteen Begay kept his water for
cooking and drinking, and a shed in which he

kept feed for his livestock. A good place. Beyond it, through a fringe of ponderosas, the morning sun had lit the rolling gray velvet of the San Juan basin. Sheep country—buffalo grass, grama, sage, chamiza, and snakeweed— punctuated by the soaring black gothic spires of Shiprock and, beyond Shiprock, 50 miles away, the smudge that marked the smokestacks of the Four Corners power plant.

Chee drank in the view, letting the grandeur of immense space lift his spirits. But something still nudged at his consciousness. Something didn't fit. In this great harmony, something was discordant.

Chee looked down at the hogan again, studying it. Bales was beside the brush arbor. The two FBI agents were out of sight—perhaps inside the death hogan, where their ignorance protected them from the malice of Gorman's *chindi.* A perfect site. It had everything. Firewood. Summer grass. Spring water for livestock in the arroyo behind the hogan. Beauty in the site and in the view. And the isolation, the sense of space, which the Pueblo Indians and whites called loneliness but the Navajos treasured. True, winters would be snowed in here, and bitter cold. The place must be well over 8,000 feet. But the hogan had been built for winter. It must have been terribly hard for the old man to abandon it. And why had he?

It was this question, Chee realized, that had been bothering him. Why hadn't the old man done what the Dinee had done for a hundred generations when they saw death approaching? Why hadn't he moved the dying Gorman out of the hogan, out under the eye of Father Sun, into the pure open air? Why hadn't he made this kinsman a death bed under the arbor, where no walls would have penned in his *chindi* when death released it, where the ghost could have lost itself in the vastness of the sky? Gorman must have died a slow, gradual death brought on by lost blood, internal damage, and infection. Death would have been nothing strange to the old man. The Navajos were not a culture that hides its people away in hospitals at their dying time. One grew up with the death of one's old people, attending death, respecting it. Begay must have seen this death coming for hours, heard it in Gorman's lungs, seen it in his eyes. Why hadn't he moved the man outside in the fashion of the People? Why had he allowed this valued homeplace to be eternally infected with ghost sickness?

Sharkey appeared in the hogan doorway and stood staring up toward Chee. Chee stared back, unseen among the boulders. Bales and the other agent were invisible now. What was the man's name? It came to him suddenly: Witry. Another thought suddenly occurred to Chee. Could the body under the rocks be Begay's? Could it be that Gorman had killed the old man? It didn't seem likely. But Chee found that his bleak mood had changed. Suddenly he was interested in this affair.

He stepped out where Sharkey could see him. "Up here!" he shouted.

Removing the rocks was quick work.

"I left the photographs in the truck," Sharkey said. "But he fits Gorman's description."

The body obviously couldn't be Hosteen Begay. Far too young. Mid-thirties, Chee guessed. It lay on the stone, face up, legs extended, arms by the sides. A plastic bread sack, its top twisted shut, was beside the right hand.

"Here's what killed him," Bales said. "Hit him right in the side. Probably tore him all up, and the bleeding wouldn't stop."

Sharkey was looking at Chee. "I guess there's no way to get a vehicle in here," he said. "I guess we'll have to carry him out to the pickup."

"We could bring a horse in," Chee said. "Haul him out that way."

Sharkey picked up the sack and opened it.

"Looks like a jar of water. And cornmeal," he said. "That make sense?"

"Yes," Chee said. "That's customary."

Sharkey poured the contents of the sack carefully out on the rock, leaving Gorman's persona to make its four-day journey into the underground world of the dead with neither food nor water. "And here's his billfold. Cigaret lighter. Car keys. Comb. Guess it was the stuff he had in his pockets." Sharkey fished through the various compartments of the wallet, laying the odds and ends he extracted on the boulder beside Gorman's knee and then sorting through them. The driver's license was first. Sharkey held it in his left hand, tilted Gorman's face toward him with the right, and made the comparison of face to photograph.

"Albert A. Gorman," Sharkey read. "The late Albert A. Gorman. Eleven thousand seven hundred thirteen La Monica Street, Hollywood, Cal." He counted quickly through the money, which seemed to be mostly hundred-dollar bills, and whistled through his teeth. "Twenty-seven hundred and forty-odd," he said. "So crime paid fairly well."

"Hey," Witry said. "His shoes are on the wrong feet."

Sharkey stopped sorting and looked at Gorman's feet. He was wearing brown low-cut jogging shoes—canvas tops, rubber soles. The shoes had been reversed, right shoe on left foot.

"No," Chee said. "That's right."

Sharkey stared at him quizzically.

"I mean," said Chee, "that's the way it's done. In the traditional way, when you prepare a corpse for burial you reverse the moccasins. Switch 'em." Chee felt his face flushing under Sharkey's gaze. "So the ghost can't follow the man after death."

Silence. Sharkey resumed his examination of the artifacts from Gorman's billfold.

Chee looked at Gorman's head. There was dirt on his forehead, and his hair was dusty from the rockfall that had buried it. But it was more than dusty. It was tangled and greasy—the hair of a man who had lain for days dying.

"Lots of money," Sharkey said. "VISA, Mastercard, California driver's license. California hunting license. Membership card in Olympic Health Club. Mug shots of two women. Coupon to get two Burger Chefs for the price of one. Social Security card. That's it."

Sharkey felt in the pockets of Gorman's jacket, unbuttoned it and checked his shirt pockets, turned the pockets of his trousers inside out. There was absolutely nothing in Gorman's pockets.

Walking back to the carryall, Chee decided he

had a second puzzle to add to the question of why Hosteen Begay had not saved his hogan from the ghost. Another piece of carelessness. Begay had in some ways prepared his relative well. Albert A. Gorman had gone through the dark hole that leads into the underworld with plenty of money he could no longer spend. No ghost could follow his confusing footprints. He had been left with the symbolic food and water for the journey. But he would arrive unpurified. His dirty hair should have been washed clean in yucca suds, combed, and braided. Boiling yucca roots takes time. Had something hurried Hosteen Begay?

> 5 <

THE BEGINNING OF WINTER bulged down out of
Canada, dusted the Colorado Plateau with
snow, and retreated. Sun burned away the
snow. The last late Canada geese appeared
along the Sun Juan, lingered a day, and fled
south. Winter appeared again, dry cold now. It
hung over the Utah mountains and sent outrid-
ers of wind fanning across the canyon country.
At the Shiprock subagency office of the Navajo
Tribal Police the wind shrieked and howled,
buffeting the walls and rattling the windows,
distracting Jim Chee from what Captain Largo
was saying and from his own thoughts about
Mary Landon. The Monday morning meeting
had lasted longer than usual, but now it was
ending. The patrolmen, shift commanders, dis-
patchers, and jailers had filed out. Chee and
Taylor Natonabah had been signaled to stay behind. Chee lounged in his folding chair in the

corner of the room. His eyes were on Largo, explaining something to Natonabah, but his mind was remembering the evening he had met Mary Landon: Mary watching him in the crowd at the Crownpoint rug auction, Mary sitting across from him at the Crownpoint Café, her blue eyes on his as he told her about his family—his sisters, his mother, his uncle who was teaching him the Mountain Way and the Shooting Way and other curing rituals of the Navajo Way, preparing him to be a *yataalii*, one of the shaman medicine men who kept the People in harmony with their universe. The genuine interest on Mary's face. And Mary, finally, when he had given her a chance to talk, telling him of her fifth-graders at Crownpoint elementary, of the difference between the Pueblo Indian children she'd taught the year before at the Laguna-Acoma school and these Navajo youngsters, and of her family in Wisconsin. He'd known, he thought now, even on that first meeting, that this white woman was the woman he wanted to share his life with.

A fresh blast of wind rattled sand against the windows and seeped through some crack somewhere to move icy air around Chee's ankles. His memory skipped ahead to the weekend he'd taken Mary back on the plateau to his mother's summer hogan south of Kayenta. When he'd asked his mother later what she'd thought of Mary, his mother had said, "Will she be a Navajo?" And he had said, "Yes, she will be." Now he knew he had been wrong. Or probably wrong. Mary Landon would not be a Navajo. How could he change that? Or, if he couldn't change it, could Jim Chee stop being a Navajo?

Now Natonabah was leaving, zipping up his fur-lined jacket, his face flushed, his mouth grim. Clearly the captain had, in his low-key way, expressed disapproval. Chee quit thinking about Mary Landon and reexamined his conscience. He'd already done that automatically when Largo had signaled him to stay behind and had thought of no violations of Largo's rules and regulations. But now Captain Largo's large round face considered him, even blander and milder than usual. Often that meant trouble. What had he done?

"You all caught up on your work?"

Chee sat up straight. "No, sir," he said.

"You catch that Yazzie who's bootlegging all that wine?"

"No, sir."

"Found that kid did the cutting on the Ute Reservation?"

"Not yet." It was going to be worse than he'd expected. He'd only had the Ute stabbing added to his case list Friday.

Largo was peering down into the file folder in which he kept Chee's reports. It was a bulky file, but Largo apparently decided to shorten the ordeal a little. He flipped rapidly through it, then closed it and turned it face down on his desk. "All this still-unfinished business then?" he asked. "You got plenty to keep your mind occupied?"

"Yes, sir," Chee said. "Plenty of work to do."

"I got the impression that you had time on your hands," Largo said. "Looking for something to keep you occupied."

Chee waited. Largo waited. Ah, well, Chee thought, might as well get it over with. "How's that, sir?" he asked.

"You pulled the file on the Gorman business," Largo said. His expression asked why.

"Just curious," Chee said. Now he would get a lecture on respecting jurisdictions, on minding his own business.

"You find anything interesting in there?"

The question surprised him. "Not much in there at all," he said.

"No reason for there to be," Largo said. "It's not our case. What were you looking for?"

"Nothing specific. I wondered who Gorman was. And who was the man who came after him. The one Gorman shot at the laundry. What Gorman was doing in Shiprock. How Begay fit in. Things like that."

Largo made a tent of his fingers above the desk top and spent a moment examining it. "Why were you curious?" he asked, without taking his eyes off his fingers. "Fight in a parking lot. The survivor runs to his kinsman to hide out and heal. Everything looks normal. What's bothering you?"

Chee shrugged.

Largo studied him. "You know," he said, "or anyway you heard from me, that an FBI agent got killed back in California in this one. The Agency is always touchy. This time they're going to be extra touchy."

"I was just curious," Chee said. "No harm done."

"I want you to tell me what made you curious."

"It wasn't much," Chee said. He told Largo about the way Gorman's corpse had been prepared, with its hair unwashed, and of wondering why Begay had not moved Gorman outside before the moment of death.

Largo listened. "You tell Sharkey about this?"

"He wasn't interested," Chee said.

Largo grinned.

"Maybe no reason to be," Chee admitted. "I don't know much about Begay. Lots of Navajos don't know enough about the Navajo way of getting a corpse ready. Lots of 'em wouldn't care."

"Younger ones, maybe," Largo said. "Or city ones. Begay isn't young. Or city. What do you know about him?"

"They call him Hosteen, so I guess the people up there respect him. That's about it."

"I know a little more than that," Largo said. "Begay is Tazhii Dinee. In fact, I'm told his aunt is the *ahnii* of that clan. He's lived up there above Two Gray Hills longer than anybody can remember. Has a grazing permit. Runs sheep. Keeps to himself. Some talk that he's a witch."

Largo recited it all in a flat, uninflected voice, putting no more emphasis on the last sentence than the first.

"There's some talk that just about everybody is a witch," Chee said. "I've heard you were. And me."

"He seems to have a good reputation," Largo said. "People up there seem to like him. Say he's honest. Takes care of his relatives." That was the ultimate compliment for a Navajo. The worse insult was to say he acted like he didn't have any relatives. In Navajo country, families come first.

Chee wanted to ask Largo why he had learned so much about an old man who kept to himself high in the Chuska Mountains. As Largo had said, the Gorman shooting was an FBI case—white-man business completely outside the jurisdiction of the Navajo Tribal Police. Instead of asking, he waited. He'd worked for Largo two years, first at the Tuba City subagency and now here at Shiprock. Largo would tell him exactly what Largo wanted him to know and all at Largo's own pace. Chee knew very little about the Tazhii Dinee—only that the Turkey People were one of the smallest of the sixty or so Navajo clans. If Begay's aunt was the clan's *ahnii*, itsmatriarch/judge/fountain-of-wisdom, then his was a most respected family and he would certainly know enough of the Navajo Way to properly prepare a kinsman for burial.

"Gorman was the son of Begay's youngest sister," Largo said. "The Bureau of Indian Affairs relocated a bunch of that clan in Los Angeles in the nineteen forties and fifties. In fact, Begay seems to have been among the few of that outfit that didn't go. I think one of his daughters also stayed. Lived over around Borrego Pass. Dead now. And a few Tazhii Dinee are supposed to have moved over to the Cañoncito Reservation. But the clan doesn't amount to much any more."

Largo walked to the window and stood, back

to Chee, inspecting the weather in the parking lot.

"We've got a girl missing from St. Catherine Indian School," Largo said. "Probably a runaway. Probably nothing much." The captain exercised the storyteller's pause-for-effect. "She's the granddaughter of Hosteen Begay. Told a friend she was worried about him. The nuns at St. Catherine called the police there at Santa Fe because they said she wasn't the type that runs away. Whatever type that is." Largo paused again, still looking at something or other in the parking lot. "Attended her morning classes on the fourteenth. Didn't show up for classes after lunch."

Chee didn't comment. The bloody business in the parking lot had happened the night of the eleventh. On the twelfth Old Man Begay had walked into the Two Gray Hills Trading Post, bought his futile bottle of aspirin, and mailed a letter. How long would it take a letter to get from Two Gray Hills to Santa Fe? Two days?

Largo walked back to his desk, found a package of cigarets in the drawer, and lit one. "The other thing," he said through the cloud of blue smoke, "is the FBI is unusually uptight about this one. Very grim. So I did some asking around. It turns out one of their old-timers got killed a couple of months ago, like I told you. He was on something that ties in with this business." Largo turned away from his parking lot inspection to gaze at Chee. "You been a cop long enough to know how it is when a cop gets killed?"

"I've heard," Chee said.

"Well, anyway, they *never* want us interfering in their jurisdiction. So think how sore they'd get if it happened when they've got an agent dead. And nobody to hang it on."

"Yeah," Chee said.

"Unfortunately," Largo said, "you're the logical one to handle this missing St. Catherine girl."

Chee let that pass. What Largo meant was that he had a reputation for being nosy. He couldn't deny it.

"You want me to be careful," Chee said.

"I want you to turn on the brain," Largo said. "See if you can pick up the girl. If you run into anything that bears on what happened to Gorman, then you back off. Tell me. I tell Sharkey. Everybody's happy."

"Yes, sir," Chee said.

Largo stood by the window, looking at him. "I really mean it," he said. "No screwing around."

"Yes, sir," Chee said.

> 6 <

THE GIRL'S NAME WAS SOSI. Margaret Billy Sosi. Age seventeen. Daughter of Franklin Sosi, no known address, and Emma Begay Sosi (deceased) of Borrego Pass. The form listed Ashie Begay, grandfather, care of Two Gray Hills Trading Post, as the "person to be notified in event of emergency." The form was a photocopy of an admissions sheet used at the Santa Fe boarding school, and there was nothing on it, or on the attached Navajo Tribal Police missing persons report form, that told Chee anything he didn't already know. He slipped the two sheets back into their folders and turned to the copies he made from the Gorman homicide report.

The wind, blowing from due north now, gusted around his pickup truck and rattled particles of parking lot debris against its door. Chee did not consciously dislike the wind. It was part of the totality of day and place, and to dislike it would be contrary to his Navajo nature. But it made him uneasy. He read quickly through the Gorman file, covering first the chronology of what had happened at the laundry and then turning to the investigating officer's transcription of his interview with Joseph Joe, looking for the oddity that had bothered him when he had first gone through the report.

"Subject Joe said Gorman had called him to the car and engaged him briefly in conversation. Joe said that as he walked away from the Gorman vehicle, the rented vehicle driven by Lerner came into the lot. . . ."

Engaged him briefly in conversation. About what? Why had Gorman driven from Los Angeles to be shot at a laundromat? It seemed to Chee that an answer to the first question might offer some clue to the answer of the second. It certainly seemed a logical question—something he would have asked Old Man Joe. Why hadn't it been asked? Chee glanced at the name of the investigating officer. It was Sharkey. Sharkey seemed smart.

Chee read through the rest of the report. Lerner had chartered a plane at a Pasadena airport, flown to Farmington, and rented an Avis car. Judging from the time elapsed, he had driven directly and rapidly to Shiprock. Looking for Gorman, obviously. How had he found him at the laundry? That could have been easy enough if he knew the car Gorman was driving. He would have been looking for it, and the highway in from Farmington passed directly by the lot where Gorman was parked. That left the question of why. The data in the report on Gorman himself made him seem trivial enough— simply a car thief. Lerner, from the report and what gossip Chee had heard, was a minor Los Angeles hoodlum. The chartered plane seemed grotesquely glossy and expensive for an incident involving such unimportant people.

Chee put the report back in its folder and looked quickly through the papers he'd picked up from his in-basket. Nothing much. A Please Return Call slip showing that "Eddie" had called about "Blue Door." Eddie pumped gas at night at the Chevron station beside the San Juan bridge. His mother was an alcoholic, Eddie did not like bootleggers, and the Blue Door Bar at the reservation boundary outside Farmington was a haunt for those who hauled beer, wine, and whiskey into the reservation's outback. Eddie meant well, but unfortunately his tips never seemed to lead anywhere.

The next memo informed all officers of the theft of a pinto mare from the Two Gray Hills Trading Post; of a pickup order on a man named Nez who had beaten his brother-in-law with a hammer at the family sheep camp above Mexican Water, and of the confirmation of identification of a middle-aged woman found dead beside the Shiprock-Gallup highway. Cause of death was also confirmed. She'd been run over by a vehicle while sprawled, unconscious from alcohol, on the pavement. Chee took a second look at the identification. He didn't know the name, but he knew the woman, and a score like her, and their husbands and their sons. He had arrested them, and manhandled them into his patrol car, and cleaned up after them, and eased their bodies onto stretchers and into ambulances. In the milder seasons, they drank themselves to death in front of trucks on U.S. 666 or Navajo Route 1. Now, with the icy wind beginning to blow, they would drink themselves to death in frozen ditches.

That wind buffeted his truck, stirring a cold draft around his face. Chee turned on the ignition and started his engine. Where was Mary Landon at this moment? Teaching her fifth-graders at Crownpoint. Chee remembered the afternoon he had stood on the walk outside the windows of her classroom and watched her—a silent pantomime through the glass. Mary Landon talking. Mary Landon laughing. Mary Landon coaxing, approving, explaining. Until one of her students had seen him standing there and looked at him, and he had fled in embarrassment.

He turned his mind away from that and rolled the pickup out of the lot. He would see Eddie about the Blue Door later. The stolen pinto mare and the angry brother-in-law and the rest of it could wait. Now the job was to find Margaret Billy Sosi, aged seventeen, granddaughter of Ashie Begay, clanswoman of a dead man whom people called Albert Gorman, who seemed to have been running, but not running fast enough or far enough. And thus the first step to finding Margaret Billy Sosi was finding Hosteen Joseph Joe and asking him the question Sharkey hadn't asked, which was what Albert Gorman had said to him at the Shiprock Economy Wash-O-Mat.

⟩ 7 ⟨

FINDING JOSEPH JOE PROVED simple enough. In cultures where cleanliness is valued and water is scarce, laundries are magnets—social as well as service centers. Chee took for granted that the people at the Shiprock Economy Wash-O-Mat would know their customers. He was correct. The middle-aged woman who managed the place provided Joseph Joe's full family genealogy and directions to his winter place. Chee rolled his patrol car southward across the San Juan bridge with the north wind chasing him, then west toward Arizona, and then south again across the dry slopes of snakeweed and buffalo grass toward the towering black spire of basalt that gave the town of Shiprock its name. It was the landmark of Chee's childhood—jutting on the eastern horizon from his mother's place south of Kayenta, and a great black thumb stuck into the northern sky during the endless lonely winters he spent at the Two Gray Hills Boarding School. It was there he'd learned that the Rock with Wings of his uncle's legends had, eons ago, boiled and bubbled as molten lava in the throat of an immense cinder cone. The volcano had died, millions of years had passed, abrasive weather—like today's bitter wind— had worn away cinders and ash and left only tough black filling. In today's bleak autumn light, it thrust into the sky like a surreal gothic cathedral, soaring a thousand feet above the blowing grass and providing—even at five miles' distance—a ludicrously oversized backdrop for Joseph Joe's plank and tarpaper house.

"I already told the white policeman about it," Hosteen Joe told Chee. Joe poured coffee into a plastic Thermos bottle cap and into a white cup with RE-ELECT MCDONALD FOR TRIBAL PROGRESS printed around it, handed Chee the political cup, took a sip from the other, and began telling it all again.

Chee listened. The wind seeped through cracks, rustling the Farmington *Times* Joe was using as a tablecloth and stirring the spare clothing that hung on a wire strung across a corner of the room. Through the only south window, Chee could see the tall cliffs of Shiprock, now obscured by blowing dust, now black against the dust-stained sky. Joseph Joe finished his account, sipped his coffee, waited for Chee's reaction.

Chee took a courtesy sip. He drank a lot of coffee. ("Too much coffee, Joe," Mary would say. "Someday I will reform you into a sipper of tea. When I get you, I'm going to make sure you last a long time.") He enjoyed coffee, respected its aroma, its flavor. This was awful coffee: old, stale, bitter. But Chee sipped it. Partly courtesy, partly to cover his surprise at what Joseph Joe had told him.

"I want to make sure I have everything right," Chee said. "The man in the car, the man who drove up first, said he wanted to find somebody he called Leroy Gorman?"

"Leroy Gorman," Joe said. "I remember that because I thought about whether I had ever known anybody by that name. Lots of Navajos call themselves Gorman, but I never knew one they called Leroy Gorman."

"The man you were talking to, his name was Gorman too. Did the white policeman tell you that?"

"No," Joe said. He smiled. "White men never tell me much. They ask questions. Maybe they were brothers."

"Probably the same family, anyway," Chee said. "But it sounds like this white policeman didn't ask you enough questions. I wonder why he didn't ask you about what Gorman said to you."

"He asked," Joseph Joe said. "I told him."

"You told him about Gorman asking you where to find Leroy Gorman."

"Sure," Joseph Joe said. "Told him the same thing I told you."

"Did you tell the policeman about the picture Gorman showed you?"

"Sure. He asked me a bunch of questions about it. Wrote it down in his tablet."

"That picture," Chee said. "A house trailer? Not a mobile home? Not one of those things that has a motor and a steering wheel itself, but something you pull behind a car?"

"Sure," Joseph Joe said. He laughed, his wrinkled face multiplying its creases with amusement. "Used to have a son-in-law lived in one. No room for nothing."

"Two things," Chee said. "I want you to remember everything you told the white policeman about the picture—everything in it. And then I want you to see if you can remember anything you didn't tell him. Was it just a picture of a trailer? Was it with a bunch of other trailers? Hitched behind a car? One man in the picture, standing there?"

Joseph Joe thought. "It was a color picture," he said. "A Polaroid." He walked to a tin trunk against the wall, opened the lid, extracted a photo album with a black cardboard cover. "Like this one," he said, showing Chee a Polaroid photo of Joseph Joe standing beside his front door with a middle-aged woman. "Same size as this," he said. "Had the trailer in the middle, and a tree sort of over it, and just dirt in front."

"Just one man in it?"

"Standing by the door. Looking at you."

"What kind of tree?"

Joe thought. "Cottonwood. I think cottonwood."

"What color leaves?"

"Yellow."

"What color trailer?"

"It was aluminum," Joe said. "You've seen 'em. Round on both ends. Round shape. Big things." Joe indicated the bigness with his hands and laughed again. "Maybe if my son-in-law had one that big, he'd still be my son-in-law."

"And the picture," Chee said. "You said he took it out of his wallet. Did he put it back in again?"

"Sure," Joe said. "Not in those little pockets where you keep your license and things. Too big for that. He put it in with the money. In the money place."

"You tell the white policeman that?"

"Sure," Joe said. "He was like you. He asked a lot of questions about the picture."

"Now," Chee said. "Did you think of anything you didn't tell him?"

"No," Joseph Joe said. "But I can think of some things I haven't told you."

"Tell me," Chee said.

"About the writing," Joe said. "On the back side it had an address written, and something else, but I couldn't see what it was. I don't read. But I could see it was something short. Just two or three words."

Chee thought about it on the way back. Why had Sharkey said nothing of the picture in his report, or of Albert Gorman trying to find Leroy Gorman? Had that part been deleted before the Navajo Tribal Police received their version? What kind of a game was the Agency playing? Or was it Sharkey's game, and not the FBI's?

"The FBI wants you," Mary said. "You impressed them at the Academy. They accepted you when you applied. They'd accept you again if you applied again. And they'd keep you close to the reservation. You'd be more valuable to them here. Why would they move you someplace else?" And he'd said something about not to count on it. Something about in Washington an Indian was an Indian, and they'd be as likely to have him working with the Seminoles in Florida, just like they have a Seminole over in Flagstaff working with the Navajos. And Mary had said nothing at all, just changed the subject. As Chee changed it now, forcing his memory away from the soreness.

He remembered Sharkey standing beside Gorman's body, Gorman's wallet in his hand, piling its contents on the boulder. No photograph of a trailer. Had Sharkey palmed it? Hidden it away? Chee's memory was excellent, the recall of a People without a written memory, who keep their culture alive in their minds, who train their children to memorize details of sand paintings and curing ceremonials. He used it now, re-creating the scene, what Sharkey had said and done, Sharkey looking into the money compartment of the wallet, removing the money, looking again, inspecting flaps and compartments: Sharkey seeking a Polaroid photograph that wasn't there.

> 8 <

THE LIGHT WAS TURNING RED. The sun had
dipped beneath the western horizon, and the
clouds in the west—dazzling yellow a few mo-
ments earlier—were now reflecting scarlet.
Soon it would be too dark to see. Then Chee
would confront his decision. He would either
walk back to his pickup truck, go home, and
write off this idea as a waste of time or he would
search the one place he hadn't searched. That
meant taking out his flashlight and stepping
through the hole into darkness. At one level of
his intellect it seemed a trivial thing. He would
crouch, step over the broken siding, and find
himself standing erect inside the abandoned
death hogan of Hosteen Begay. To the Jim Chee
who was an alumnus of the University of New
Mexico, a subscriber to *Esquire* and *Newsweek*,
an officer of the Navajo Tribal Police, lover of
Mary Landon, holder of a Farmington Public

Library card, student of anthropology and sociology, "with distinction" graduate of the FBI Academy, holder of Social Security card 441-28-7272, it was a logical step to take. He had repeated the long, bumpy drive into the Chuskas, made the final two-mile trudge from his pick-up to this place, to see what he could find at this hogan. How could his logical mind justify not searching it?

But "Jim Chee" was only what his uncle would call his "white man name." His real name, his secret name, his war name, was Long Thinker, given him by Hosteen Frank Sam Nakai, the elder brother of his mother and one of the most respected singers among Four Corners Navajos. Since he had gone to Albuquerque to study at the University of New Mexico, he did not often think of himself as Long Thinker. But he did now. He stood on the talus slope above where he had found the Gorman corpse looking down at the Begay hogan as a Navajo would look at it. The east-facing door was boarded shut. (He had resealed it before he'd left, repairing the damage done by Sharkey.) The smoke hole was plugged. The *chindi*, which had left the body of Gorman at the moment of Gorman's death, was trapped inside—a summation of all in the dead man's life that was evil and out of harmony with the Navajo Way.

Everything in Long Thinker's training conditioned him to avoid *chindis*. "If you have to be out at night, go quietly," his mother had taught him. "The *chindis* wander in the darkness." And his uncle: "Never speak the name of the dead. Their *chindi* thinks you are calling it." He had come to terms with these ghosts in high school and reduced them to rational terms at the university, converting them into something like the dietary taboos of Jews and Moslems, the demons of Christians. But from this talus slope, in the dying light, in the dead stillness of this autumn evening, the rationality of the university was canceled.

And there was another side to all this. "You did it," Mary Landon would say. "When you stepped through that corpse hole, you proved that you can be a Navajo on an emotional plane but an assimilated man intellectually." And he would say, "No, Mary, you simply don't understand," and she would say . . .

He turned away from that and considered what he'd learned. Almost nothing. He'd driven straight from the place of Joseph Joe and started his work here with a meticulous examination of the hogan yard. He'd learned that Hosteen Begay used his sweat bath more than most, that he kept goats as well as sheep, and that he owned two horses (one newly shod).

Recent additions to Begay's garbage dump included an empty lard can, an empty Shurfine flour sack, and tin cans that had held peaches, creamed corn, and pork and beans. The garbage told him that Begay dipped snuff (an addiction unusual among Navajos), that he did not use beer, wine, or whiskey, and (judging from the discarded Dr. Scholl's footpads) that he suffered from bunions. None of that was helpful.

Nor had he found anything helpful in the second stage of his hunt, an equally careful sweep up and down the arroyo behind the hogan and around the wooded slopes above and below Begay's little meadow. He simply confirmed what he'd learned on his original inspection. Begay had, as would be expected of any prudent shepherd, taken his flocks to downhill pastures weeks ago, before early winter storms could trap them. And when he'd abandoned this place, he'd ridden the newly shod horse and led the other, heavily loaded. He'd headed downhill, probably for some shortcut he knew to reach the road to Two Gray Hills. Maybe, Chee thought, he could follow those tracks far enough to get some hint of his destination. But that seemed wildly unlikely. Time, wind, and the dry season made tracking doubtful, and even if he could track, his work would also certainly simply lead him to the road to the trading post.

Today's wind had been the sort any tracker hates—dry and abrasive, blasting sand against the face and erasing signs. But it had died away in late afternoon, and now the total calm of an autumn high-pressure area had settled over the high country. From his place on the talus slope Chee could see, across Begay's empty homestead, a hundred miles to the southeast all the way to the dark blue bump on the horizon that was Mount Taylor, Mary Landon's favorite mountain. (Now Mary would be finished with her school day, finished with her supper, out for her evening walk—sitting someplace, probably, looking at it from much closer quarters. Chee could see her vividly, her eyes, the line of her cheek, her mouth. . . .)

Old Man Begay had taken time to clean out his hogan and pack his stuff on his horses. Why hadn't he taken the time to collect the few yucca roots required to make the suds to wash his kinsman's hair? What had hurried him? Had it been fear? An urgent need to attend to some duty? Chee stared down at the homestead, trying to visualize the old man smashing with his ax at the broken wall where the corpse hole was formed, destroying what must have been important to him for much of his life.

Then he heard the sound.

It came to him on the still, cold air, distant but distinct. It was the sound of a horse. A whinny. The sound came from the arroyo—from the spring or from Begay's corral just beyond it. Chee had been there two hours earlier and had spent thirty minutes establishing from tracks and manure that no animal had been there for days. Nor was this the season for open range grazing this high in the mountains. Livestock had been taken, long since, to lower pastures, and even strays would have moved downhill, out of the intense morning cold. Chee felt excitement growing. Ashie Begay had come home to collect something he'd forgotten.

The horse was exactly where Chee expected it to be—at the spring. It was an elderly pinto mare, roan and white, fitting the description of the one stolen from Two Gray Hills. It wore a makeshift rope halter on its ugly hammer head. Another bit of rope secured it to a willow. Hardly likely that Hosteen Begay, who owned horses of his own, would have taken it. Who had? And where was he?

The night breeze was beginning now as it often did with twilight on the east slope of mountains. Nothing like the morning's dry gusts, but enough to ruffle the mare's ragged mane and replace the dead silence with a thousand little wind sounds among the ponderosas. Under cover of these whispers, Chee moved along the arroyo rim, looking for the horse thief.

He checked up the arroyo. Down the arroyo. Along the ponderosa timber covering the slopes. He stared back at the talus slope, where he had been when he'd heard the horse. But no one could have gotten there without Chee seeing him. There was only the death hogan and the holding pen for goats and the brush arbor, none of which seemed plausible. The thief must have tied his horse and then climbed directly up the slope across the arroyo. But why?

Just behind him, Chee heard a cough.

He spun, fumbling for his pistol. No one. Where had the sound come from?

He heard it again. A cough. A sniffling. The sound came from inside Hosteen Begay's hogan.

Chee stared at the corpse hole, a black gap broken through the north wall. He had cocked his pistol without knowing he'd done it. It was incredible. People do not go into a death hogan. People do not step through the hole into darkness. White men, yes. As Sharkey had done. And Deputy Sheriff Bales. As Chee himself, who had come to terms with the ghosts of his people, might do if the reason was powerful enough.

But certainly most Navajos would not. So the horse thief was a white. A white with a cold and a runny nose.

Chee moved quietly to his left, away from the field of vision of anyone who might be looking through the hole. Then he moved silently to the wall and along it. He stood beside the hole, back pressed to the planking. Pistol raised. Listening.

Something moved. Something sniffed. Moved again. Chee breathed as lightly as he could. And waited. He heard sounds and long silences. The sun was below the horizon now, and the light had shifted far down the range of colors to the darkest red. Over the ridge to the west he could see Venus, bright against the dark sky. Soon it would be night.

There was the sound of feet on earth, of cloth scraping, and a form emerged through the hole. First a stocking cap, black. Then the shoulders of a navy pea coat, then a boot and a leg—a form crouching to make its way through the low hole.

"Hold it," Chee said. "Don't move."

A startled yell. The figure jumped through the hole, stumbled. Chee grabbed.

He realized almost instantly he had caught a child. The arm he gripped through the cloth of the coat was small, thin. The struggle was only momentary, the product of panic quickly controlled. A girl, Chee saw. A Navajo. But when she spoke, it was in English.

"Turn me loose," she said, in a breathless, frightened voice. "I've got to go now."

Chee found he was shaking. The girl had handled this startling encounter better than he had. "Need to know some things first," Chee said. "I'm a policeman."

"I've got to go," she said. She pulled tentatively against his grip and relaxed, waiting.

"Your horse," Chee said. "You took her last night from over at Two Gray Hills."

"Borrowed it," the girl said. "I've got to go now and take her back."

"What are you doing here?" Chee asked. "In the hogan?"

"It's my hogan," she said. "I live here."

"It is the hogan of Hosteen Ashie Begay," Chee said. "Or it was. Now it is a *chindi* hogan. Didn't you notice that?"

It was a foolish question. After all, he'd just caught her coming out of the corpse hole. She didn't bother to answer. She said nothing at all, simply standing slumped and motionless.

"It was stupid going in there," Chee said. "What were you doing?"

"He was my grandfather," the girl said. For the first time she lapsed into Navajo, using the noun that means the father of my mother. "I

was just sitting in there. Remembering things."
It took her a moment to say it because now tears
were streaming down her cheeks. "My grandfather would leave no *chindi* behind him. He was
a holy man. There was nothing in him bad that
would make a *chindi.*"

"It wasn't your grandfather who died in
there," Chee said. "It was a man named Albert
Gorman. A nephew of Ashie Begay." Chee
paused a moment, trying to sort out the Begay
family. "An uncle of yours, I think."

The girl's face had been as forlorn as a child's
face can be. Now it was radiant. "Grandfather's
alive? He's really alive? Where is he?"

"I don't know," Chee said. "Gone to live with
some relatives, I guess. We came up here last
week to get Gorman, and we found Gorman had
died. And that." Chee pointed at the corpse hole.
"Hosteen Begay buried Gorman out there, and
packed up his horses, and sealed up his hogan,
and went away."

The girl looked thoughtful.

"Where would he go?" Chee asked. The girl
would be Margaret Sosi. No question about
that. Two birds with one stone. One stolen pinto
mare and the horse thief, plus one missing St.
Catherine's student. "Hosteen Begay is your
mother's father. Would he . . . ?" He remem-

bered then that the mother of Margaret Billy
Sosi was dead.

"No," Margaret said.

"Somebody else then?"

"Almost everybody went to California. A long
time ago. My mother's sisters. My great-grand-
mother. Some people live over on the Cañoncito
Reservation, but . . ." Her voice trailed off, became suddenly suspicious. "Why do you want to
find him?"

"I want to ask him two questions," Chee said.
"This is a good hogan here, solid and warm, in
a place of beauty. Good firewood. Good water
for the cattle. Enough grass. Hosteen Begay
must have seen that his nephew was dying. Why
didn't he do as the People have always done and
move him out into the air so the *chindi* could go
free?"

"Yes," Margaret Sosi said. "I'm surprised he
didn't do that. He loved this place."

"I have heard Hosteen Begay lived the Navajo
Way," Chee said.

"Oh, yes," Margaret said. "My grandfather always walked in beauty."

"He would have known how to take care of a
corpse then? How to get it ready for its journey?"

The girl nodded. "He taught me about that.

About putting a little food and water with the body. And things it needs for four days."

"And what you do so the *chindi* will not follow it?"

"Oh, yes," she said. "After you make the yucca suds and wash the hair, you reverse the shoes." She pantomimed the act of switching. "So the *chindi* will be confused by the footprints." As she finished the sentence her voice trailed off, and she glanced at the corpse hole, the irregular broken doorway into the darkness of the hogan. She looked, and Chee felt her shiver under his hand. Seventeen, by the record, he thought, but she looks about fifteen.

"I wouldn't have gone in there if I had known it wasn't Grandfather." She looked up at Chee. "What do I have to do? What can you do when you've been where you catch the ghost sickness? How do I get rid of the *chindi?*"

"You're supposed to take a sweat bath," Chee said. "And as soon as you can you have a sing. Tell your family about it. They'll call in a Listener, or a Hand Trembler, to make sure you have the right ceremonial. Usually it would be part of the Night Way, or the Mountaintop Way. Then your family will hire a singer, and . . ." It was occurring to Chee that Margaret Sosi didn't have much family to depend on for such familial duties. "Is there somebody who can do that for you?"

"My grandfather would do it," she said.

"Anyone else? Until we find him?"

"I guess just about everybody went to Los Angeles," she said. "A long time ago."

"Look, Margaret," Chee said. "Don't worry about it. Let me tell you about *chindi*. Do you know much about religion?"

"I go to a Catholic school. We study religion."

"A lot of religions have rules about what not to do, what not to eat, things like that. The Koran tells the Moslems not to eat pigs. When the wise men were writing that, a lot of diseases were spread by eating pork. It was smart to avoid it. Same with some of the Jewish rules about foods. Most religions, like us Navajos, have rules against incest. You don't have intercourse within your own family. If you do, inbreeding makes bad stock. And with us, Changing Woman and Black God taught us to stay away from where people have died. That's wise too. Avoids spreading small-pox, bubonic plague fleas, things like that."

Even in the twilight, Chee could see Margaret's face was skeptical.

"So the ghost is just disease germs," she said.

"Not exactly," Chee said. "There's more to it than that. Now we know about germs, so when we violate the taboo about a death hogan we know how to deal with any germs we might catch. But we also know we've violated our religion, broken one of the rules the People live by. So we feel guilty and uneasy. We no longer have *hozro*. We no longer live in beauty. We're out of harmony. So we need to do what Changing Woman taught us to do to be restored in the Navajo Way."

Margaret's expression was slightly less skeptical. "Did you go in there?"

"No," Chee said. "I didn't."

"Are you going to?"

"Only if I have to," Chee said. "I hope I don't have to." The answer surprised him. He had avoided the hogan, and the decision, all afternoon. Suddenly he understood why. It had something to do, a great deal to do, with Mary Landon—with remaining one of the Dinee or with stepping through into the white man's world.

"I would break the taboo because it is my job," he said. "But maybe it won't be necessary. You stay right here. I've got a lot of questions I need to ask you."

The hole had been made by chopping the logs forming part of the lower wall of the hogan away from the frame that held them. Chee aimed his flashlight through the hole. In the center, directly under the smoke hole, five partly burned logs lay on the hearth, their charred ends pointing neatly inward. Just beside the hearth, Begay's cooking stove stood, a heavy cast-iron affair that he must have taken apart to haul in. Nothing else had been left behind. A clutter of cardboard boxes lay near the boarded east entrance with a red Folger's coffee can standing near them. Except for that, the packed earthen floor was bare. Chee swung the flash around, examining the walls. Wooden crating had been fashioned into shelving on both sides of the east entrance and a wire was strung along the south wall, about chest high. Chee guessed Begay had hung blankets across it, screening off about a third of the hogan's floor space for privacy. He let the beam of the flashlight drift along the logs, looking for anything that might have been left in the crevices. He saw nothing.

He switched the flash back to the cardboard cartons. Obviously Sharkey and Bales had examined them. Must have. No reason for him to go inside. What would he do if he went in? Run his fingers between the logs. Poke into cracks. Looking for what? There was no reason to go inside. No reason to step through the hole into the darkness. What would he tell Margaret Sosi to make her believe that?

As soon as he turned away from the hole, into the redder darkness of the dying twilight, he realized he wouldn't have to answer that question. Margaret Sosi was gone.

"Margaret!" he shouted. He exhaled through his teeth, a snorting sound expressing anger and disgust. Of course she was gone. Why wouldn't she be? Gone with the important questions left unanswered. Unasked, in fact, because he, in his shrewdness, had left them for the last, until the girl had time to come to trust him. The obvious questions.

Why did you run away from school, run to your grandfather's hogan, steal a horse in your hurry to get here? Why did you tell your friend at St. Catherine you were worried about your grandfather? What did you expect to find here? What did you hear? How did you hear it?

Chee stared out into the darkness, seeing nothing but the shape of trees outlined against the night sky. She couldn't be far, but he would never find her. She would simply sit down and wait, silently, while he floundered around. He could walk within six feet of her and not see her unless she betrayed herself with panic. With Margaret Sosi, he thought, there was no chance of that whimper of fear, that panicky movement that would betray concealment. She was young and thin, but Chee had seen enough to respect her nerve. He remembered the quick control of fear when he'd grabbed her. The quick tug to test his grip. Margaret Sosi would not lose her courage.

And tonight, she'd need it. The air against his cheek was already icy. In the thin, dry air here, 9,000 feet above sea level, the temperature would drop another 30 degrees before sunrise.

Chee cupped his hands and shouted toward the mountain slope. "Margaret. Come back. I won't arrest you."

He listened, waiting for the echo to subside, and heard nothing.

"Margaret. I'll take you wherever you want to go."

Listened again. Nothing.

"I'm leaving the horse. Take it back where you got it. Find a warm place."

Again, silence.

On his way back to the pickup, Chee detoured down into the arroyo and jammed his lunch sack between the willow limbs where the mare's halter was tied. One of his two bologna sandwiches was left in it, and an orange. The mare snorted and rubbed against his shoulder, wanting company as much as food.

> 9 <

JIM CHEE WAS ABOUT two thirds of the way through his account of what he had seen and heard at the places of Hosteen Joe and Hosteen Begay when Captain Largo raised his large brown hand, palm out, signaling a halt. Largo picked up the telephone, got the switchboard.

"Call Santa Fe. St. Catherine Indian School. Get me that sister I talked to earlier. The principal. Tell her I need to talk to that friend of the Sosi girl. Need some more information from her. See if you can get me that girl on the telephone. Ring me back when you get her. Okay?"

Then he turned back to Chee and heard the rest of it without comment or question. His black eyes watched Chee without expression, drifting away now and then to study his thumbnail, then back to study Chee.

"First piece of advice I need from you," he said when Chee had finished, "is what to tell

Sharkey when he finds out the Navajo Tribal Police have been questioning one of his witnesses in a federal murder case."

"You mean Joseph?"

"Of course, Joseph," Largo said, shifting his eyes from thumbnail to Chee. "I don't have any trouble explaining why you went to Begay's hogan. You went there looking for a runaway girl, and Sharkey has to swallow that one because you're lucky, as usual. She was there."

"Tell him I talked to Joseph for the same reason," Chee suggested.

"Doesn't work."

"I guess not," Chee admitted. "Change the subject then. Ask him why the Agency left that stuff out of the report they sent you. Ask him why no mention was made of Gorman coming to Shiprock looking for somebody else named Gorman. Ask him why the picture of the trailer . . ." Chee didn't finish the sentence. Largo's expression said he wasn't liking this suggestion.

"What am I going to tell Sharkey?" he repeated. "Are you going to give me an explanation, or do I have to tell him that one of our men violated department regulations and the direct and specific orders of his commanding officer and is therefore being suspended without pay to teach him some better manners?"

"Tell him the *girl* disappeared right after all

this happened, and she's Hosteen Begay's granddaughter and we think—"

The telephone interrupted him. Largo picked it up. "Good," he said. "What's her name again?" He listened, then pushed the selector button.

"Miss Pino? This is Captain Largo of the Navajo Tribal Police in Shiprock. Could you give us a little more information to help us find Margaret Sosi? . . . What? . . . No, no, we think she's all right. What we need is a clearer idea of just why she left when she did."

Largo listened.

"A letter?" he said. "When? . . . Did she say anything about what her grandfather said in it? . . . Uh-huh. I see. Did she mention the name? . . . Sure. I can understand that. Would you remember it if you heard it? Was it Gorman? . . . You're sure. How about the first name . . . Her uncle? . . . Okay. Go over it again, would you please? Everything you remember she said."

Largo listened, jotting notes now and then on his pad.

"Well, thank you very much, Miss Pino. This is very helpful. . . . No, we think she's safe enough. We just want to find her." Largo looked at Chee with no expression whatever and added, "Again."

"One other thing. Did she say when she

planned to come back? . . . Okay. Well, thanks again."

Largo replaced the receiver, gently.

"You are one lucky Navajo," he said, "which is almost as good as being smart."

Chee said nothing.

"It turns out I can tell Sharkey that Margaret Sosi got a letter from her grandfather mailed the day after the shooting, and in this letter he told her about some danger. Warned her to stay away from Shiprock and not to go around Gorman."

"Danger?"

"That's all she told the Pino girl. Or all the Pino girl could remember her saying about it. She said Margaret told her her grandfather must be very upset, because writing a letter was very hard for him to do. She said she was worried about him and she was going to see about him."

"That was the letter he mailed from Two Gray Hills," Chee said.

"Probably," Largo said. "Been nice if you'd have asked her some things like that. Something practical. You know, Sharkey's going to be curious about that. He's going to say, 'Now, your policeman had this girl in his custody. But he didn't ask her why she came to the hogan. Or find out about the letter. Or find out that her grandfather warned her about something dangerous. Or anything useful.' And Sharkey is going to say, 'What do your officers chat about in cases like this? I mean, how do they keep the conversation going until they let the suspect walk away?' What do I tell Sharkey about that?"

"Tell him we talked about ghosts," Chee said.

"Ghosts. Sharkey will enjoy that."

"I heard you asking the Pino girl if Margaret Sosi mentioned a first name for Gorman," said Chee, changing the subject. "You thinking the same thing I am?"

"I'm thinking we don't know for sure which Gorman she was supposed to stay away from. The one who had already been shot or the one that one was looking for."

"The occupant of the aluminum house trailer," Chee said.

"Maybe," Largo said. He scratched his nose. "Or maybe he was just having his picture taken." He got up, stretched, walked to the window, and scrutinized the parking lot. "Put it together," he said, finally, "and what have you got? Albert Gorman, a car thief, drives from L.A. to Shiprock, looking for Leroy Gorman. A minor hoodlum rents himself an expensive plane ride and comes after Albert. They shoot each other. Gorman goes to his uncle's place, gets there in the night, tells the old man what happened. Next day Uncle Begay goes out to the trading post and mails a letter to Margaret Sosi. Tells her something or other is dangerous and to stay away from Shiprock and to stay away from Gorman. Which Gorman? I'd guess it wouldn't be the Gorman with the bullet in him. Old as Begay was, he's seen enough hurt people to know when one's bad hurt. He'd have known Albert wasn't dangerous to anybody. The warning would be about Leroy. Stay away from Leroy."

"Yes," Chee said. "Probably, anyway."

Largo abandoned the parking lot and sat again behind his desk. He regained his interest in his thumbnail, holding the heel of his hand on the desk top, thumb rampant, flexing slowly when he inspected it. "I am going to call Sharkey," he said. "I think we better find that Sosi girl." He glanced from thumb to Chee. "Again," he added.

"Yes," Chee said. "I think so."

"And Leroy Gorman," Largo said. "You think Sharkey has that photograph? Of the trailer?"

"No." Chee described Sharkey's search of Albert Gorman's wallet.

"So either Gorman got rid of the photograph or somebody else took it out of his wallet. Old Man Begay, maybe. Or Joseph Joe didn't know what the hell he was talking about."

While he was saying that, Largo was picking up his telephone. He told the operator to call the FBI in Farmington and get Sharkey for him. "You sure Joe told Sharkey about the photograph, about Albert Gorman looking for Leroy Gorman?"

"I'm sure."

"That son of a bitch," Largo said. He didn't mean Joe.

Sharkey was in.

"This is Largo," Largo said. "We have a teenage girl missing, which looks like it's tied in with this Gorman shooting of yours. Name's Margaret Billy Sosi. You heard anything we should know about?"

Largo listened.

"She's a student at St. Catherine Indian School in Santa Fe. Granddaughter of Ashie Begay. She got a letter he mailed the day after the shooting. Her granddaddy told her something about staying away from Shiprock and not to go around Gorman because it was dangerous."

Largo listened.

"I don't know why," he said, and listened again. "Well, it was worth a call anyway," he said. "She cut out from school after she got the letter and went up to the Begay place. We were puzzled about why old Ashie Begay would think

Gorman was dangerous when he had a bullet in him—dying right there in the hogan, you know. Could there be another Gorman the old man was talking about?"

Largo listened very briefly.

"We can't ask her because"—he glanced at Chee—"she got away and disappeared again. What? Granddaughter. Margaret Sosi is Ashie Begay's granddaughter. You guys got anything that would point us to looking for another Gorman around here? A dangerous one?"

Largo listened again. He covered the mouthpiece with his palm, looked at Chee, said, "Lying son of a bitch," and listened some more.

"Well," he said, "we went out and talked to Joseph Joe to see if Albert Gorman had said anything to him, and he told us that Albert was looking for a guy named Leroy Gorman." Largo winked at Chee. "I guess Joe forgot to tell you about that. And Joe said Gorman showed him a photograph of an aluminum house trailer, which was where this Leroy Gorman was supposed to be living. You know anything—"

Largo looked slightly surprised. "All right," he said. "We'll keep in touch."

He hung up, looking suspiciously at the telephone and then at Chee.

"Sharkey tells me that Joe didn't say anything to them about Albert Gorman looking for anybody, or about a picture, and that there was no picture on Gorman's body."

"Interesting," Chee said,

"Wonder what's going on," Largo said. "I don't think Sharkey's lying just to keep in practice."

"No," Chee said. He was thinking that he would start hunting the aluminum house trailer.

"I think we better see if we can find that house trailer," Largo said.

> 10 <

FINDING AN ALUMINUM TRAILER in Shiprock, New Mexico, required only persistence. The town is the most populous of the hundreds of dots that mark populated places on the vastness of the Navajo Big Reservation. Even so, it counts less than 3,000 permanent residents. Knowing the trailer was parked under a cottonwood tree simplified the search. On the arid Colorado Plateau, cottonwoods grow only along streams, or beside springs, or in places where the runoff from snowmelt augments their water supply. In and around Shiprock, natural cottonwood habitat was limited to the San Juan river bottom and a few places along Salt Creek Wash and Little Parajito Arroyo. Chee checked the San Juan first, working upstream from the old U.S. 666 highway bridge and then downstream. He found hundreds of cottonwoods, and scores of places where a trailer might be parked, and dozens of trailers of all descriptions, including aluminum. Just before noon, he found an aluminum trailer parked under a cottonwood. It had taken a little less than two hours.

It was parked perhaps a mile below the bridge, near the end of a dirt track which led behind the Navajo Northern District Health Clinic, went past a pump station of the Shiprock town water system, and finally petered out on a low bluff overlooking the San Juan River. Chee parked just off the track and inspected his discovery.

The glossy metal reflected a pattern of sun and shadow in streaks caused by the bare branches above. Nothing on the ground indicated occupancy—neither litter nor the boxes, barrels, broken furniture, cots, or other effluvia of life that those who occupy trailers or hogans or other crowded spaces tend to leave outside to make room inside. There was nothing on the ground except a yellow mat of fallen cottonwood leaves.

Chee was instantly aware of this departure from the normal, as he always was of any deviation from the harmony of the expected. He noticed other peculiarities too. The trailer looked new, or almost new. Its glossy skin was clean and polished. Trailers that housed Shiprock Navajos and those who lived among them would more typically have the look of second-, third-, and fourth-hand models, wearing the dents, scrapes, and rust marks of hard wear and poor maintenance. Second, Chee noticed the trailer was tied to two black wires, telephone and electric power. The powerline was no surprise, but telephones were relatively rare on the reservation. The Navajo telephone book, which covered more territory than all the New England States and included Hopi country as well as Navajo, was small enough to fold neatly into one's hip pocket, and nearly all the numbers in it were for some sort of government or tribal office or a business. Residential telephones were unusual enough to draw Chee's attention.

He took off his uniform jacket and hat and put on his nylon windbreaker. As he walked toward the trailer he became aware that the telephone was ringing. The sound was faint at first, muffled by distance and whatever insulation the walls of such trailers held, then louder as he came nearer. It rang as if it had always been ringing, as if it would ring on through the noon hour, and into the evening, and forever. Chee stopped at the retractable metal step below the trailer door, hesitated, then tapped on the metal. The telephone's ring coincided with the knock. He waited, knocked again into the silence, listened. No response. He tried the knob. Locked.

Chee walked away from the trailer and stood beside the cottonwood's trunk, thinking. Below, on a path leading down to the riverbank and along it, a man was walking. He was whistling, coming up the path toward Chee. He wore neatly fitted denims, a long-sleeved shirt of blue flannel, a denim vest, and a black felt hat with a feather jutting from its band. When the path tilted upward so that Chee could see his face, he recorded a man on the young side of middle age, clean-shaven, slender, distinctly Navajo in bone, with a narrow, intelligent face. He walked with an easy grace, swinging the heavy stalk of a horseweed like a cane. He walked now through a tunnel of sunlit yellow where the willows and alders arching over the path had not yet lost all their foliage, still not seeing Chee. But suddenly, he heard the persistent summons of the telephone bell.

He dropped the stick and sprinted for the trailer, hesitating when he noticed Chee, then regaining stride.

"Got to catch the phone," he said as he ran past. He had his key out when he reached the door, unlocked it deftly, scrambled inside. Chee stood at the steps by the open door, waiting.

"Hello," the man said, and waited. "Hello.

Hello." He waited again, then whistled into the speaker. "Anybody home?" He waited, then whistled again, waited again, watching Chee. Whoever had dialed his number had apparently put down the phone and left it to ring. "Hello," the man repeated. "Anybody there?" This time he seemed to receive an answer.

"Yes, this is Grayson. . . . Well, I wasn't far. Just went for a walk down the river." Then he listened. Nodded. Glanced at Chee, his expression curious. "Yes," he said. "I will." He leaned his hip against the trailer's cooking stove and reached into a drawer to extract a note pad and pen. "Give it to me again." He wrote something. "All right. I will."

He hung up and turned to face Chee.

Chee spoke in Navajo, introducing himself as born to the Slow Talking Clan, born for the Bitter Water People, naming his mother and his deceased father. "I am looking for a man they call Leroy Gorman," he concluded.

"I don't understand Navajo," the man said.

Chee repeated it, clan memberships and all, in English. "Gorman," the man said. "I don't know him."

"I heard he lived here. In this trailer."

The man frowned. "Just me here," he said.

Chee was conscious that the man hadn't identified himself. He smiled. "You're not Leroy Gorman then," Chee said. "Is that a safe bet?"

"Name's Grayson," the man said. He stuck out his hand and Chee shook it. A hard, warm grip.

"Wonder how I got the wrong information," Chee said. "This is the place." He gestured at road, tree, river, and trailer. "Supposed to be an aluminum airflow trailer like this. Strange."

Grayson was studying Chee. Behind his smile his face was stiff with tension, the eyes watchful.

"Who is he, this Gorman? Who told you he lived here?"

"I don't really know him," Chee said. "I was just supposed to deliver a message."

"A message?" The man stared at Chee, waiting.

"Yeah. To Leroy Gorman."

The man waited, leaning in the doorway. Past him Chee could see dishes beside the sink, but except for that the interior of the trailer was utterly neat. The man was a Navajo, Chee was sure of that from his appearance. Since he didn't speak the language, or pretended not to, and since he didn't follow Navajo courtesy, he might be a Los Angeles Navajo. But he said he wasn't Leroy Gorman.

"You're the second person to show up today looking for this Gorman guy," he said. He laughed, nervously. "Maybe Gorman himself will show up next. You want to leave that message with me so I can pass it along if he does?"

"Who was the first one?"

"A girl," Grayson said. "Cute little skinny girl. Late teens."

"She tell you her name?"

"She did. I can't think of it."

"How about Margaret? Margaret Sosi."

"Yeah," Grayson said. "I think so."

"How little? How was she dressed?"

"About so," Grayson said, indicating shoulder height with a gesture of his hand. "Thin. Wearing a blue coat like in the navy."

"What did she want?"

"Seemed to think I was this Gorman. And when she understood I wasn't, she wanted to ask me about her grandfather. Had he been here. Things like that. Don't remember his name. She wanted to find this Gorman because he was supposed to know something about where her grandfather was." Grayson shrugged. "Something like that. Didn't make much sense."

Chee put his foot on the step, shifted his weight. He wanted the man to invite him inside, to extend the conversation. Who was Grayson? What was he doing here?

"Maybe I could leave that message," he said. "You got a place I could write it down?"

Grayson hesitated a heartbeat. "Come on in," he said.

He provided a sheet from his note pad and a ballpoint pen. Chee sat on the built-in couch beside the table and printed, in a large, slow hand:

LEROY GORMAN—
ALBERT GOT KILLED. GET IN TOUCH WITH
CHEE AT

He hesitated. The tribal police switchboard operator responded to calls with "Navajo Tribal Police." Chee imagined Grayson hearing that and hanging up, his curiosity satisfied. He wrote in the number of the Shiprock Economy Wash-O-Mat and added:

LEAVE MESSAGE.

Chee didn't look up while he printed. He wanted Grayson to be reading the message—and he was sure that he had. He folded the paper, and refolded it, and wrote on the final fold:

FOR LEROY GORMAN, PRIVATE.

He handed it to Grayson.

"Appreciate it," Chee said. "If he does show up."

Grayson didn't look at the note. His face was tense. "Sure," he said. "But it ain't likely. Never heard of him until that girl showed up."

"Did she say where she was going when she left?"

Grayson shook his head. "Just said something about going off to find some old woman somewhere. Didn't mean much to me."

It didn't mean much to Jim Chee either, except that finding Margaret Sosi probably wouldn't be easy.

> 11 <

FINDING MARGARET SOSI, Chee thought, would take a lot more time and hard work than finding an aluminum trailer under a cottonwood tree. Maybe she'd gone to Los Angeles. Maybe she hadn't. Chee remembered himself at seventeen. Easy enough to talk about Los Angeles, and to dream about it, but for a child of the reservation it represented a journey into a fearful unknown—a visit to a strange planet. He could never have managed it by himself. He doubted if Margaret Sosi would have taken that long and lonely leap into God-knew-what. More likely she was hunting Old Man Begay on the Big Reservation. Maybe she was tracking down members of their clan who'd moved to the Cañoncito. That was exactly what Chee would begin doing. Unfortunately, members of the Turkey Clan seemed to be scarce.

But Chee's route back to his office led past the

intersection of U.S. 666 and Navajo Route 1. The 7-Eleven store there served as depot for both Greyhound and Continental Trailways. It would only take a minute to check, and Chee took it. A middle-aged Navajo named Ozzie Pete managed both the store and bus ticket sales. No. No tickets had been sold to Los Angeles for weeks. Maybe months. For the past several days he was dead sure he had sold no tickets at all to a skinny teenage girl in a navy pea coat.

From his office, Chee called south to the trading posts at Newcomb and Sheep Springs. Same questions. Same answers. He called Two Gray Hills. The mare was back in the corral, neither better nor worse for its abduction, but no one had seen anyone who looked like Margaret Sosi. So much for that.

Chee tilted his chair back against the wall and crossed his boots on his wastebasket. What now? He had no idea how to start looking for Turkey Clan people. It could only be purely random. Driving around, stopping at trading posts, chapter houses, watering points, every place where people collected, to ask questions and leave word. Sooner or later someone would either be Turkey Clan or know someone who was. And since the Turkey Clan was virtually extinct it would more likely be later rather than sooner before he made connections. Chee did not feel lucky. He dreaded the job. But the only alternative to starting it was to see if he could think of an alternative.

He thought.

What had Margaret done when she slipped away from him at the hogan? Taken the mare back to Two Gray Hills, obviously. Before that she had, perhaps, taken time to take a sweat bath. Hosteen Begay's sweat bath was handy and in plain view from where she'd tied the mare. Perhaps she had made sure Chee was gone, built a fire, heated the stones, poured spring water over them, and cleansed herself in the healing steam to rub away Gorman's ghost. Chee himself had taken a steam bath in his trailer home—putting his frying pan, superheated on the stove, on the floor of his shower and pouring boiling water from his teakettle onto the hot metal to create an explosion of steam. He'd felt limp, very clean, and generally better when he'd finished his rubdown. The same would have been true of Margaret. Say she'd taken the bath, ridden the mare down to U.S. 666 and turned it loose to find its way back to Two Gray Hills, and then caught an early-morning ride back into Shiprock. Then she'd gone to Grayson's trailer looking for Leroy Gorman. How the devil had she found it? Perhaps Hosteen Begay had told her where it was when he wrote her, warning her away from Gorman. More proof that Margaret Sosi didn't scare easily. Not when her grandfather was involved. Chee thought some more. Perhaps this explained what had happened to the Polaroid photograph. Perhaps Hosteen Begay had taken it from the dying Albert Gorman and mailed it to Margaret. Whatever was on that photograph had brought Albert Gorman racing to Los Angeles to find Leroy Gorman. Would Hosteen Begay use it to keep Margaret away? The Margaret Sosi who didn't scare?

Chee sighed, took his feet down, and reached for the telephone. Maybe she *had* gone to L.A., scary as it seemed to him. Anyway, until he knew for sure, he had a reason not to start hunting elsewhere.

By midafternoon Chee knew everything about bus schedules from Shiprock southward toward Gallup and westward through Teec Nos Pos, including who drove which bus and where they lived. He knew that one Greyhound driver didn't remember having a skinny Navajo girl in a pea coat as a passenger yesterday, and another Greyhound driver was still out on his run and incommunicado. The very first Continental Trailways driver he reached made all this beside the point.

"Yeah," he said. "She flagged me down north

of the Newcomb Trading Post. She wanted a ticket to Los Angeles, but she didn't have enough money."

"How much did she have?"

"She had enough to get to Kingman, right there on the California border, and forty cents left over."

"Describe her to me," Chee said.

The driver described Margaret Billy Sosi. "Nice-looking kid," he concluded, "but she looked like she needed some fattening up and her face washed. Looked wore out. What are you fellas after her for?"

"Trying to keep her from getting hurt," Chee said.

Chee called the station at Kingman. The LA-bound bus from points east had arrived on schedule and departed, also on schedule, about fifteen minutes ago. Had anyone noticed a small, thin, tired Navajo girl with black eyes and black hair getting off? She was wearing a navy pea coat and her face needed washing. No one had noticed.

Chee called the Kingman police station, identified himself, and asked for the watch commander. He got a Lieutenant Monroney and described Margaret Sosi for what seemed to be the eleventh time. "I guess she'd be hitchhiking," Chee said. "She's trying to get to Los Angeles."

"And the bus got in when, quarter hour ago? And she's seventeen?"

"Seventeen but looks fifteen. Small."

"Pretty girl?"

"I guess so," Chee said. "Yeah. Kind of thin but she looks okay. Would have needed to have her face washed, though."

"We'll look for her," Monroney said. "And I'll call the California Highway patrol across the line and give them the word. But don't count on anything. A boy, he'd still be out there thumbing. Girl, pretty girl, that age—she'd be picked up. Long gone. But we'll look. Give me your number. We find her, we'll call. Just want her held for runaway, that it? No crime?"

"No crime," Chee said. "But there's a homicide in the background. Just keep her safe."

But maybe it was already too late for that.

> 12 <

THE "ELEVEN THOUSAND SEVEN HUNDRED THIR-
TEEN La Monica Street" address Sharkey had
read from Albert Gorman's driver's license
translated into a single-story U-shaped building
of faded pale-green stucco. Chee parked his
pickup behind an aging Chevy Nova with an
off-color fender and looked the place over. The
building seemed to house ten or twelve small
apartments, with the one on the left end of the
U wearing a small sign that said MANAGER. Attached to that, a cardboard placard proclaimed
VACANCY.

Chee walked up the narrow pathway to the
porch in front of the manager's apartment. Beside the door, opposite the vacancy sign, another
sign listed apartment occupants. Chee found no
Albert Gorman, but the name slot beside number 6 was empty. He cut across the weedy ber-
muda grass to the entrance porch of number 6,
rang the bell, and waited. Nothing. A mailbox

was mounted beside the door, its lid closed. Chee rang the bell again, listened to the buzz it produced inside the apartment, and, while he listened, pushed open the lid of the mailbox.

Two envelopes were in it. Chee moved his body to shield what he was doing from the direction of the manager's office and extracted the envelopes. One was addressed to OCCUPANT and the other to Albert Gorman. It seemed to be a telephone bill, postmarked two days earlier. Chee dropped both envelopes back into the box, rang the bell again, then tried the door. Locked. Again he shielded the action with his body because he was aware that someone was watching him. A woman, he thought, but he'd only had a momentary glimpse of the form standing behind the partly pulled curtain of the office window.

Chee turned from the door and recrossed the weedy lawn. He rang the office manager's doorbell, waited, rang it again, waited again. He glanced at his watch. What could the woman be doing? He rang the bell again, watched the second hand of his watch sweep around a full minute, and then another. The woman did not intend to come to the door. Why not? She had an apartment to rent. He rang the bell again, waited another minute, then turned and started toward his truck.

He heard the door open behind him.

"Yes?"

Chee turned. She held the door halfway open. She was as tall as Chee, gaunt, and gray—a bony, exotic face which showed Negro blood and perhaps Chinese.

"My name's Jim Chee," Chee said. "I'm looking for a man named Albert Gorman. In apartment six, I think."

"That's right," the woman said. "Apartment six is Gorman."

"He's not in," Chee said. "Do you have any idea where I could find him?"

"I think he'll be back in a little while," the woman said. "You wait. There's a chair there on his porch." She gestured across the lawn. "Just make yourself comfortable."

The accent was marked. Spanish? Probably, but not the sort of Mexican Spanish Chee heard around the reservation. Filipino, perhaps. Chee had heard there were lots of Filipinos in Los Angeles.

"Do you know when he'll be back? Actually, I'm trying to find some of his relatives. Do you—"

"I don't know anything," the woman said. "But he'll be right back. He said if anyone came looking for him to just have them wait. It wouldn't be long."

"I'm a policeman," Chee said, extracting his credentials and showing her. "I'm trying to locate a girl. About seventeen. Small. Thin. Dark. An Indian girl. Wearing a navy pea coat. Has she been here?"

The woman shook her head, expression skeptical and disapproving.

"It would have been early this morning," Chee said. "Or maybe late last night."

"I haven't seen her."

"Does Albert Gorman have any other address you know about? Where he works? Any relatives I could check with?"

"I don't know," the woman said. "You wait. You ask him all that."

"I have a friend looking for an apartment," Chee said. "Could I look at the one you have vacant?"

"Not ready yet. Not cleaned up. Tenant still has his stuff in it. You wait." And with that she closed the door.

"All right," Chee said. "I will wait."

He sat in the chair on the porch of number 6 and waited for whatever his visit here had triggered to start happening. He made no effort to calculate what that might be. The woman, obviously, had called someone when she saw him on Gorman's porch. Apparently she had been told to keep him there, and so she had stalled.

He would stay partly because he was curious and partly because there was no other choice. If he drew a blank here, he knew of no promising alternatives. This address was his only link to the Turkey Clan and Margaret Sosi. Unfortunately, the chair was metal and uncomfortable.

He got up, stretched, sauntered across the grass, fingers stuck in the back pockets of his jeans, sending the woman who was surely watching from behind the curtain the signal of a man killing time. He walked down to the street and looked up and down it. Across from him, a neon sign over the entrance of a decaying brick building read KOREAN GOSPEL CHURCH. Its windows were sealed with warped plywood. Next door was a once-white bungalow with a wheelless flatbed truck squatting on blocks before its open garage door. Once-identical frame houses stretched down the block, given variety now by age, remodeling projects, and assorted efforts to make them more livable. The line terminated in a low concrete block building on the corner which, judging from the sign painted on its wall, was a place where used clothing was bought and sold. In general, it was a little worse than the street Chee had lived on as a student in Albuquerque and a little better than the average housing in Shiprock.

Gorman's side of La Monica Street was of a

similar affluence but mostly two-story instead of one. Below his U-shaped apartment house were two more, both larger and both badly needing painting. Up the street, the remainder of the block was filled by a tan stucco building surrounded by lawn and a chain-link fence. Chee ambled along the fence, examining the establishment.

On the side porch, five people sat in a row, watching him. They sat in wheelchairs, strapped in. Old people, three women and two men. Chee raised a hand, signaling greetings. No reaction. Each wore a blue bathrobe: four white heads and one bald one. Another woman sat in a wheelchair on a concrete walk that ran just inside the fence. She, too, was old, with thin white hair, a happy smile, and pale blue vacant eyes.

"Hello," Chee said.

"He's going to come today," the woman said. "He's coming."

"Good," Chee said.

"He's going to come today," the woman repeated. She laughed.

"I know it," Chee said. "He'll be glad to see you."

She laughed again, looking happily at Chee through the fence. "Got shore leave," she said. "He's coming."

"Wonderful," Chee said. "Tell him hello for me."

The woman lost interest in him. She backed her wheelchair down the walk, humming.

Chee strolled along the fence, looking at the five who lined the porch. This was a side of white culture he'd never seen before. He'd read about it, but it had seemed too unreal to make an impression—this business of penning up the old. The fence was about six feet high, with the top-most foot tilted inward. Hard for an old woman to climb that, Chee thought. Impossible if she was tied in a wheelchair. Los Angeles seemed safe from these particular old people.

He turned the corner and walked past the front of the place. SILVER THREADS REST HOME, a sign on the front lawn said. Here there were flowers—beds of marigolds, petunias, zinnias, and blossoms of the mild coastal climate that Chee could not identify. Banks of flowers flourishing safe from the old people.

Silver Threads occupied the entire end of the block. Chee circled it, glancing at his watch, killing time. He turned into the alley separating the rest home from Gorman's apartment complex and walked down it toward Gorman's porch. He'd used up almost ten minutes.

A man, bent and skinny, was standing inside the fence watching him approach with bright blue, interested eyes. He was standing in a waist-high aluminum walking frame, its four legs planted in the grass.

"Hello," Chee said.

"You Indian?" the man asked. He had trouble with "Indian," stopping mid-word, closing his eyes, exhaling breath, trying again until he pronounced it.

"Yes," Chee said. "I'm Navajo."

"Indian lives there," the man said. He removed a hand from the walker and gestured toward Gorman's apartment.

"Do you know him?" Chee asked.

The old man struggled for words, shook his head, sighed. "Nice," he said finally. "Talks."

Chee smiled. "His name is Albert Gorman. That the one?"

The man was frowning angrily. "Don't smile," he said. "Nobody talks to me but that . . ." His face twisted with a terrible effort, but he couldn't manage the rest of it. "Him," he said finally and looked down at his hands, defeated.

"It's a good thing to be friendly," Chee said. "Too many people never have time to talk."

"He's not home," the man said. Chee could see he wanted to say something else, and waited while his fierce will struggled with his stroke-blighted mind, making it work. "Gone," he said.

"Yes," Chee said. "He has an uncle who lives

on the Navajo Reservation. In New Mexico. He went back there to visit him." Chee felt a twinge of guilt when he said it, as he always did when he was being deceptive. But why tell the old man his friend was dead?

The old man's expression changed. He smiled. "Kin?"

"No," Chee said. "But we're both Navajos, so we're kin in a way."

"He's in bad trouble," the man said, clearly and plainly. Whatever short circuit of nerve tissue impeded his speech, it seemed to come and go.

Chee hesitated, thinking like a policeman. But what was required here was not the formula in the police manual.

"Yes, he is. I don't understand it, but when he left here someone went after him. Very bad trouble."

The old man nodded, wisely. He tried to speak, failed.

"Did he tell you about it?"

The man shook his head in the negative. Thought. Canceled the denial with a shrug. "Some," he said.

A little round woman in a tight, white uniform was approaching across the lawn. "Mr. Berger," she said, "time for us to start or we'll miss our lunch."

"Shit," Mr. Berger said. He grimaced, picked up the walking frame carefully, and pivoted.

"Don't talk dirty," the round woman said. "If we were in a wheelchair like we should be, I could push you." She glanced at Chee, found him uninteresting. "That would save us time."

"Shit," Mr. Berger said again. He moved the walking frame up the lawn, stumbling along inside it. The round woman walked behind, silent and relentless.

Only the angle of the morning sun had changed on the porch of Gorman's apartment. Chee sat in the metal chair beside the door and thought of Mr. Berger. Then he thought about Grayson: who he might be, and what Grayson was doing in Shiprock, and how he might be connected with this odd business. He tried to guess what might have caused Albert Gorman's confusion about who lived in the aluminum trailer—if in fact it was confusion. And try as he did to avoid it, he thought about Mary Landon. He wanted to talk to her. Immediately. To get up and go to a telephone, and have her called out of her classroom at Crownpoint, and hear her voice: "Jim? Is everything all right?" And he would say . . . he would say, "Mary, you win." No, he wouldn't say it that way. He'd say, "Mary, you're right. I'm going to send in the application for the FBI job. And when I hang up this telephone, I'm going to walk right to my truck and drive directly, without stopping, to Crownpoint, and that will take me about twelve hours if I don't get stopped by the highway patrol for speeding, and when I get there, you have your bags packed, and tell the principal to get a substitute teacher, and . . ."

A white Ford sedan pulled up behind his pickup truck. Two men in it. The one on the passenger side got out and hurried up the walk to the manager's office. He was a short man, middle-aged, with a stocky, disciplined body and a round pink face. He wore gray pants and a seersucker coat. The door of the office opened before he reached it. The conversation there was brief. The short man looked over at Chee, saw him, and came directly across the grass toward him. At the Ford, the driver's door opened and a much larger man emerged. He stood for a moment watching. Then he, too, came sauntering toward the Gorman apartment.

The short man was talking before he reached the porch. "Lady says you're looking for Albert Gorman. That right?"

"More or less," Chee said.

"That your truck?"

"Yes."

"You from Arizona?"

"No," Chee said. He had bought the license plates when he was stationed at Tuba City, before his transfer to Shiprock.

"Where you from?"

"New Mexico."

The bigger man arrived. Much bigger. Six-foot-four or so, Chee guessed, and broad. Much younger too. Maybe thirty-five. He looked tough. While he waited on the porch, Chee had decided he might expect FBI agents to arrive. These men were not FBI agents.

"You're a long way from home," Shortman said.

"Nine hundred miles," Chee agreed. "You fellows know where I can find this Albert Gorman? Or any of his family? Or his friends?"

"What's your connection with Gorman?" Shortman asked.

"Don't know him," Chee said. "What's your interest?"

Under Shortman's coat, Chee could see just the edge of a brown leather strap, which might be part of a harness holding a shoulder holster. Chee couldn't think of anything else it might be. Shortman wasn't interested in answering Chee's question. He reached under his jacket and extracted a leather folder from the inside pocket. "Los Angeles Police Department," he said, letting the folder flop open to display a badge and photograph. "Let's see some identification."

Chee fished out his wallet, opened it to show his own badge, and handed it to Shortman.

"Navajo Tribal Police," Shortman read. He eyed Chee curiously. "Long way from home," he said again.

"Nine hundred miles," Chee repeated. "And now can you tell me anything about this Gorman? We have a girl—" He stopped. The big man was engulfed in laughter. Chee and Shortman waited.

"Mister," the big man said, "Shaw here can tell you everything about Albert Gorman. Shaw is the world champion expert on everything about Gorman. Gorman is part of Shaw's hobby."

Chee held out his hand to the short man. "My name is Chee," he said.

"Willie Shaw," the short man said, shaking hands. "This is Detective Wells. You have time for a talk? Cup of coffee?"

Wells shook Chee's hand with the soft, gentle grip he'd learned to expect from huge people. "Good thing Shaw is retiring," he said. "Police work is starting to interfere with the hobby."

"Mr. Chee here will give me a ride, I'll bet," Shaw said. "We'll go to that Vip's down on Sunset." He said it to Wells, but Wells was already walking back to the Ford. "Now," Shaw said, "I want you to start off by telling me what got the Navajo police interested in Albert Gorman."

Chee kept the explanation simple—just the oddity of Gorman's unfinished burial preparations, the question of where Hosteen Begay had gone, the problem of finding Margaret Sosi and learning from her what Begay had said in his letter. He had finished it by the time they slid into a booth in the coffee shop. Shaw stirred sweetener into his coffee. It was time for questions.

"The way I got it, Lerner just drove up to Gorman in the parking lot and shot him. Gorman shot back and drove off. Lerner dead in the lot. The Feds find Gorman dead of his gunshot wound later, at his uncle's house. That's it?"

"Not quite," Chee said. He filled in the details.

"And Albert had stopped in the lot to talk to an old man there?"

"Yes," Chee said. "To ask directions." Apparently Shaw had seen the FBI report. Why would he have seen it?

Wells had driven into the Vip's lot and come in and spotted them.

"Scoot over," he said, and sat beside Shaw.

"What did they talk about?" Shaw asked. "Gorman and the old man?"

It was exactly the right question, Chee thought. Shaw impressed him.

"What's your interest in Gorman?" Chee asked, keeping his voice very friendly. "I mean, as a Los Angeles police department detective?"

"In fact, as an arson squad detective," Wells said. "It's a good question. One of these days, the captain is going to ask it. He's going to say, Sergeant Shaw, how come everybody is burning down Los Angeles and you're chasing around after car thieves?"

Shaw ignored him. "I'd like to find out exactly why Gorman went to New Mexico," he said. "That would be interesting."

"You going to tell me what I need to know about this end? Help me find the Sosi girl?"

"Of course," Shaw said. "But I need to know what's behind the Navajos sending a man a thousand miles outside his jurisdiction. It's got to be better than a runaway teenager."

"They didn't send me," Chee said. "I'm taking vacation time. Sort of on my own. Makes it simpler."

Wells snorted. "Lordy," he said. "Spare me from this. Two of them in the same booth. The vigilantes ride again."

"My friend here," said Shaw, tilting his round, red face toward Wells, "thinks police should just stick to their assignments."

"Like arson," said Wells. "Right now we're supposed to be over on Culver looking into a warehouse fire, which is every bit as much fun as a New Mexico homicide and which the taxpayers are paying us for."

"You're on your own then?" Shaw said. "Nothing official. A personal interest?"

"Not exactly," Chee said. "The department wants to find the girl, and Old Man Begay. They're more or less missing. And me doing it on time off makes it less complicated." Chee could see Shaw understood the implications of that.

"Yeah," Shaw said. "It's an FBI case." Some of the caution had left his face, and there was a touch of friendliness there now. And something else. Excitement?

"You were going to tell me what Gorman talked about in the parking lot," Shaw said.

Chee told him.

"Albert was looking for Leroy?" Shaw frowned. "Had a picture of a house trailer?" He extracted a leather-covered notebook from a pocket of his coat, put on his bifocals, and read.

"Joseph Joe," he muttered. "I wonder why he didn't tell the Feds about that."

"He did," Chee said.

Shaw stared at him.

"He told the FBI everything I've told you."

Shaw digested that. "Ah," he said. "So."

"If that interests you," Chee said, "you might like to know that when the FBI emptied out Albert Gorman's pockets, the photograph Gorman had shown Joe wasn't there."

"Stranger and stranger," Shaw said. "What happened to it?"

"Two obvious possibilities. Gorman threw it away after he got shot. Or Old Man Begay took it."

Shaw was reading his notebook. "I suspect you thought of a third possibility," he said, without looking up.

"That the FBI agent palmed it?"

Shaw glanced up from his notebook, a look that mixed appraisal and approval.

"I'm almost certain that didn't happen. I found the body. I was watching. He didn't have a chance."

"Could you find that trailer? Albert thought it was in Shiprock. Isn't that a small place?"

"We found it. The man living in it said his name was Grayson. Said he didn't know any Leroy Gorman."

"Do you know who Leroy Gorman is?" Shaw asked.

"That's one of the things you were going to tell me."

"Let me see that identification again."

Chee dug out his ID folder and handed it to Shaw. Shaw studied it, memorizing the information, Chee guessed. "I'll make a telephone call," he said. "Back in a minute."

Chee sipped his coffee. Through the window came the sound of traffic, the clamor of an ambulance hurrying somewhere. Wells slid his cup back and forth across his saucer, pushing it with a finger.

"He's a good man, Shaw," he said. "Great record. But he's going to screw himself up with this. Mess around until he gets into trouble."

"Why? Why's he so interested?"

"His friend got killed," Shaw said. "Died, actually." He drained the cup and signaled a waitress for a refill. "However it was, Shaw thinks they killed him, and they're getting away with it. It drives him crazy."

"He's not happy with the investigation?"

"There isn't any," Wells said. He waited for the waitress to finish pouring. "The man had a coronary. Natural causes. No sign of foul play."

"Oh."

Wells's face was moody. "I've been his partner for four years, and I can tell you he's a dandy. Three commendations. Smart as they get. But he can't seem to turn loose of this Upchurch business."

"Upchurch. Was he the FBI agent?"

Wells stared at him.

"I heard the FBI lost a man on this case," Chee explained. "And they seem to be acting funny."

"They're going to be acting even funnier when they find out Shaw—" He stopped. Shaw slid back into the booth.

"Albert Gorman was a car thief," Shaw began without preamble. "He and Leroy. They're brothers, and they both stole cars for a living. Worked for an outfit called McNair Factoring. Old outfit down on the San Pedro docks. Imports coffee beans, cocoa, raw rubber, stuff like that—mostly from South America, I think, but some from Asia and Africa too. Exports whatever is going out—including stolen cars. It's sort of a specialty. Mostly expensive stuff. Ferraris, Mercedes, Caddies. So forth. Mostly to Argentina and Colombia, but now and then to Manila and wherever they had orders. That's the way they worked. Gorman and the others were on commission. They'd get orders for specific models. Say a Mercedes Four-fifty SL. And a delivery date when the right ship was at the wharf. They'd spot the car, wait until the date, then nail it and drive it right onto the dock. Have it on the ship before the owner missed it. Pretty slick."

Shaw paused to see if Chee agreed. Chee nodded.

"Then an FBI agent got into this. His name

was . . . Kenneth . . ." Shaw's voice choked. The muscle along his upper jaw tensed. Wells, who had been watching him, looked quickly away to study the traffic passing on this seedy end of Sunset Boulevard. Chee thought of the Navajo custom of not speaking the name of the dead. For Shaw, the name had certainly called back the ghost.

Shaw swallowed. "His name was Kenneth Upchurch." He stopped again. "Sorry," he said to Chee. "He was a good friend. Anyway, Upchurch worked up a case on the McNair operation. A good one."

Shaw had control again now. A man who had made a thousand reports was making another one, and he made it clearly and concisely. When had gone to the grand jury he found his witnesses slipping away. A first mate fell overboard. A ship's captain remained behind in Argentina. A thief lost his memory. Another changed his mind. Upchurch got some indictments, but the top people got away clean."

"Went scot-free," Wells said sourly. "A pun. The clan McNair went scot-free. Ha ha." He didn't smile and neither did Shaw. A bad old joke.

"That was nine years ago," Shaw continued. "After a while McNair Factoring went back into the car business, and Upchurch got wind of it, and the word was they were tying it in now with Colombia cocaine trade. He told me that what went wrong the first time was that everybody knew about it. This time he was going to make a case by himself. Keep it totally quiet. Just work on it by himself; you know, take his time. Nail a witness here and there and keep 'em in the bag until he was ready. Tell nobody except whoever he had to work with in the U.S. District Attorney's office, and maybe somebody in Customs if he had to. So that's the way he did it. Worked for years. Anyway, this time he had everything cold. He was really tickled, Ken was." Shaw's red face was happy, remembering it. "He had witnesses nailed down to tie in the top people, old George McNair himself, and a guy named Robert Beno, who sort of ran the stealing end, and one of McNair's sons—everybody big."

Shaw gestured with both hands, a smoothing motion. "Like silk. Seven indictments. The whole shebang." Shaw grinned at the recollection. "That was on a Tuesday. Complete surprise. Got 'em all except Beno, mugged and fingerprinted and booked in and bonded out on Wednesday. Kenneth, he made some of the arrests himself—McNair, it was, and his boy—and then he made sure he got his witnesses tucked in safe. He had 'em in the Witness Protection Program, and as soon as they got through talking to the grand jury, he'd take 'em himself and tuck 'em back in. Not taking any chances this time. By that weekend he was all finished with it."

Shaw stopped, staring straight ahead. He took a deep breath and let it out.

"That weekend, Saturday night, we was going to celebrate. My wife and Kenneth and Molly. Had reservations. Saturday he was driving down the Santa Monica Freeway. Don't know where he was going, but he was just about at Culver City, and he lost control of the car and hit a van and another car and went over an off ramp."

There was another dragging moment of silence.

"Killed him," Shaw said.

Wells stirred, started to say something, shrugged instead.

"How?" Chee asked. "In the crash?"

"Autopsy showed he had a coronary," Shaw said, glancing at Wells. "Death by natural causes."

"Nice timing," Chee said.

"Sure, it makes you suspicious," Wells interjected. "It made the FBI suspicious too. One of their own had just closed a big case. They got right on it, heavy. I know for sure they had the autopsy rechecked. Had their own doctor in on it. They didn't find anything but a guy driving down the freeway having a heart attack."

"The FBI," Shaw said. "Lawyers and certified public accountants."

"LAPD Homicide helped them," Wells said. "You know that. You know those guys as well as I do. Better. They don't miss much when they're interested, and they didn't find a damn thing either."

"Well," Shaw said, "you know and I know that McNair killed him. Just killed him to get even. Had money enough to do it so it wouldn't show. Induced the heart attack."

Wells looked angry. Obviously it was something they had covered before. Often. "Nothing wrong with the brakes. No sign of drugs in the body. No skin punctures. No poison darts fired from airplanes. No canisters of poison gas. Nothing in the blood."

"The car was all torn up," Shaw said. "So was the body."

"They're used to that," Wells said. "The pathologists—"

"We won't argue about it," Shaw said. "Kenneth is dead. He was as good a friend as a man ever had. I don't want somebody getting away with killing him, casual as swatting a fly."

"What's the motive?" Chee asked.

Shaw and Wells both looked at him, surprised.

"Like I said, getting even," Shaw said. "For starters. And it got him out of the way before the trial."

"But the D.A.'s office would handle that, wouldn't it? Was he an important witness?"

"I guess not," Shaw conceded. "But the case was his baby. He'd be in the background, making sure nothing went wrong, making sure the witnesses were okay, that the prosecutor knew what the hell he was doing. That sort of thing."

"Witnesses all safe?"

"Sure. Far as I know, and I think I would have heard. But it's the Witness Protection Program. All secret, secret, secret."

"Albert Gorman wasn't safe," Chee said.

"Albert wasn't a witness," Shaw said. "Kenneth couldn't turn him. Couldn't get anything on him. Leroy, now, he's a witness. Ken got him cold, in a stolen Mercedes with his hotwire kit and keys. And he even had written himself a note about the model and when to deliver it to what dock. Two previous convictions."

"So now Leroy's a protected witness?" Chee said.

"I'd guess yes," Shaw said. "Wouldn't you? I know he hadn't been in town since before the grand jury. If I was guessing, I'd guess maybe they assigned him the name of Grayson and hid him in a trailer on the Navajo Reservation."

"So why shoot Albert?" Chee asked. But he was already guessing the answer.

"I don't think they planned to do it. I think they were watching him to see if he'd lead 'em to Leroy, and they followed him to Shiprock. Sent Lerner. Lerner was supposed to follow Al or get him to tell where Leroy was hiding. Something went wrong. Boom."

"Makes sense," said Chee. "The FBI report didn't say much about Lerner. Who was he?"

"We have a folder on him," Shaw said. "Long-time hood. Used to work in one of the longshoremen's rackets, extortion, collecting for the sharks. Then he was bodyguard for somebody in Vegas, and for a long time he worked for McNair."

"Sort of a hit man?" Chee asked. He was uneasy with the expression. It wasn't a term in the working vocabulary of the Tribal Police.

"Not really," Shaw said. "Their regular muscle, from what Upchurch told me, was a freelancer. A guy named Vaggan."

"Wonder why he didn't go," Chee said. "Looks like it would have been important to them."

Shaw shrugged. "No telling. Maybe it cost too much. Vaggan is supposed to be expensive."

"But good," Wells said. "But good."

> 13 <

VAGGAN RARELY WASTED TIME. Now, while he waited for 3 A.M. and time to begin Operation Leonard, he listened to Wagner on his tape deck and reread *The Navajo*. He sat in the swivel chair in the rear of his van, light-tight curtains drawn over its windows, and absorbed the chapter about Navajo curing ceremonials. The page he read was illuminated by a clip-on battery-powered light that Vaggan had ordered from *Survive* magazine at a cost of $16.95 plus COD charges. He kept the light in the glove box of the van for just such occasions, the long waits in dark places where he had business to do and where he didn't want to be noticed. The light was advertised for reading in poorly lit motels, on aircraft, and so forth, and it made turning pages awkward. But its light focused narrowly on the page and nowhere else. If anyone was snooping around Vaggan's van they'd see nothing reflecting on his windshield.

It wasn't likely that anyone would be outside. The Santa Ana had started blowing early in the afternoon. It was blowing harder now, and Vaggan had picked this place carefully—the screened off-street parking apron outside the four-car garage of a massive, colonial-style mansion on Vanderhoff Drive. The owners of the mansion were elderly, their only live-in servant a middle-aged woman. The light went off early, and the parking area offered Vaggan an unobtrusive place to wait, out of sight of the Beverly Hills police patrol. The patrol prowled the streets at night looking for those, like Vaggan, who had no legitimate after-hours business here among the richest of the rich.

In addition, it was near enough to Jay Leonard's home to make it convenient for Vaggan to scout his grounds. He had done that at 11 P.M., and again a little after midnight, and twice since midnight. And it was far enough from Leonard's to reduce the risk of being noticed in the event someone else was watching. Vaggan had considered that possibility—as he considered all possibilities when he took on a job—but it didn't seem to be happening. Leonard seemed to be content to base his safety on a triple line of defense. He had a rent-a-cop staying in his home with him, he'd installed a fancy new burglar alarm, and he'd rented two guard dogs.

Vaggan found the thought of the dogs intruding into his concentration. The paragraph he'd just read concerned the taboo violations which could be counteracted by the Enemy Way ceremonial, a subject that interested him mildly. But the thought of the dogs excited him. He had inspected them (and they had inspected him) on each of his scouting trips. Dobermans. A male and a female. The dog man at Security Systems, Inc., had assured him that the dogs were trained not to bark, but Vaggan had wanted to check that out. Even with the Santa Ana blowing, even with the whine and howl of the wind covering just about every sound, Vaggan didn't want the animals raising a clamor. Leonard was a drinker, and a coke snorter, and Leonard might be out of it. But he would be nervous. So might the rent-a-cop.

"You can ask Jay Leonard," the dog man said. "He's had 'em better'n a week now and they ain't barked for him. If they'd been bothering his neighbors, I don't think he'd have recommended us to you."

"Maybe they haven't had any reason to be barking," Vaggan said. "But what if somebody walks along the fence there with a dog on a leash, or a cat, or if somebody wants to come through the gate. What if a cat gets in the yard?"

"No barking," the man said. "One kind of

watchdog, you teach him to bark when some-body shows up. Encourage it when they're pups. Another kind of guard dog, attack dog, you don't want barking. You teach 'em right away they bark they get punished for it. Before long, nothing makes 'em bark. We can rent you a pair like that."

Vaggan had reserved two dogs for December, long after he'd be finished with Leonard. He used a name and address he'd picked out of the Beverly Hills telephone book and paid a $50 deposit to make sure the man would know the deal was made and wouldn't be calling Leonard about the barking business. Leonard was into the Man for $120,000, not counting interest and Vaggan's collection fee. And Vaggan's collec-tion fee—usually 15 percent—was going to be a lot fatter this time.

"Publicity," the Man had said. "That's what we need. You know what that silly little bastard said to me? What Leonard said? He said don't give him any of that crap about breaking knee-caps. Them days is past, he said. He said take him to court. Did I know you couldn't collect a gambling debt in court?"

Vaggan had just listened. The Man was very, very angry.

"I said I'd turn it over to my collection, and he

said screw my collection. He said try to get tough with him and I'd end up in the pen."

"So you want a kneecap broken?"

"Something or other," the Man said. "Whatever is appropriate. But I want people to know about it. Too many deadbeats saying sue me. Let's get some publicity out of Leonard. Cut down on the bad debts."

"Whether or not we get the money?"

"I don't mean kill him," the Man said. "Kill him, I'm out a hunnert and twenty grand and interest. He ain't gonna name me in his will."

Vaggan didn't respond to that. He sat easily in the telephone booth, receiver to his ear, and watched a woman trying to back a Cadillac into a space at the shopping center across the street. He let the silence tick away. Better to let the Man start the next phase of the negotiations.

"Vaggan," he said at last. "There'd be a bonus for the publicity."

"I can see that," Vaggan said. "What you're asking me to do is sort of challenge the cops to do something about it. Roughing up Leonard is one thing. Roughing him up so it's public is like daring 'em to catch me. And if I do it right, I'm putting myself out of the collection business. All you have to do is mention Jay Leonard and they hand you a cashier's check."

"What's fair?" the Man asked.

"I'd say all of it," Vaggan said. "You lose the Leonard money but you make the point with everybody else. All of it, if I really do it right. I mean, make the TV news shows, and the *Times*. Get a big splash."

They argued for a while, haggling, each man objecting. But they settled on a price. Several prices, actually, depending on the nature of the publicity and on Leonard paying up promptly. Even the lowest one was enough to pay for putting in the reinforced concrete storage house that Vaggan was going to build into the hillside next to his place. It made the lost $50 dog deposit seem reasonable.

Vaggan glanced at his watch. Twelve minutes now. He put down the book. The wind gusted against the van, shaking it on its springs and battering it with a barrage of twigs and whatever the dry Santa Ana gale picked up from the lush lawns of Beverly Hills. The sound of *Götterdämmerung* muttered from the speakers—turned low in the interest of safety but, at this thunderous point in the opera, loud enough to be heard over the storm. The passage always moved Vaggan. The Twilight of the Gods, the end of the decayed old order, the cleansing. Blood, death, fire, chaos, honor, and new beginnings. "Nietzsche for thought, Wagner for music," his father would say. "Most of the rest of it is for niggers." His father . . .

He turned his thoughts instantly from that, glanced at the watch again. He would leave a little early. He slipped off his shoes, pulled the chest-high waders from their box, and slipped his legs into them, the splint on his left forefinger making the action clumsy. Vaggan hated the splint for reminding him of his moment of carelessness. But the finger had healed quickly, and he'd soon be done with the bandage. Meanwhile, he'd not think about it. "Think about your strength," the Commander had said. "Forget weaknesses." The waders were heavy with the equipment he had stuffed in their pouch. He pulled the rubber over his hips and adjusted the suspenders. Even in the waders he was graceful. Vaggan exercised. He ran. He lifted weights. He weighed 228 pounds, and every ounce of it was conditioned to do its job.

Vaggan picked up the canvas airline bag he used to carry his bulkier equipment, locked the van behind him, and walked slowly up the sidewalk, getting accustomed to the clumsy waders. At the corner, the view opened before him. The lights of Los Angeles, bright even at 3 A.M., spread below. Vaggan thought of a luminescent southern sea, and then of the phosphorescence of decay. An apt thought. He shuffled along on the waders' felt soles, keeping silent, keeping in the shadows, looking at the glow of sleeping Los Angeles. The glow of a rotting civilization. One day soon it would be sterilized, burned clean. Very soon. The article he'd clipped from *Survival* estimated fourteen Soviet warheads targeted on the Greater Los Angeles area, including LAX, the port at Long Beach, and the city center, and the attendant military installations and industrial areas. Hydrogen bombs. They would clean the valley. When it was over, and safe again, he could climb these hills at night and look down into clean, quiet darkness.

The dogs heard him coming or perhaps—despite the wind—smelled his scent. They were waiting for him at the fence. He examined them while he extracted his wire cutter and his pipe wrench from the wader pouch. The dogs stared back, ears forward, tense and expectant. The smaller one, the female, whined, and whined again, and made a quick move toward the wire, drawing her lips back in a snarl. The Santa Ana had blown clouds and smog out to sea, as it always did, and there was enough late moon to reflect from white, waiting teeth. Vaggan pulled on his heavy leather gauntlets and snipped the first wire. The dogs wouldn't bark. He was sure of that now.

He had made sure on his second visit to the

fence, taking along the cardboard box with the cat in it. The cat was a big Siamese tom which Vaggan had adopted at the Animal Shelter in Culver City—paying $28 to cover the cost of license, shots, and neutering. The dogs had charged the fence, standing tense, and the cat had smelled them. He had scratched and struggled inside the box so frantically that Vaggan had to put it on the ground and hold the lid down with one hand while he cut the cord holding it. Then he had thrown the box over the fence.

The cat had emerged in midair. It landed running and lasted a minute or so. Vaggan had wanted to learn if the dogs' training to silence would hold even during the excitement of an attack. It had. They had killed the cat with no more sound than their breathing. He had also learned something useful about how they worked. The female was the leader. She struck, and then the big male went in for the kill. Instinct, probably. It hardly seemed to Vaggan that it was something animals could be taught.

Vaggan's sentiments, oddly for him, had been with the cat. For the cat was the foredoomed loser in this affair, and Vaggan had no regard for losing, or for those who did it. Vaggan, however, admired cats, respected their self-sufficient independence. He identified with that.

Often, in fact, he thought of himself as a cat. In the world that would come after the missiles and the radiation he would live as a predator, as would everyone who survived more than a week or so. Cats were first-rate predators, requiring no pack to hunt, and Vaggan found them worthy of his study.

Vaggan had started clipping wires at the bottom of the fence, wanting to be standing erect when he had cut enough to make it possible for the dogs to attack. But the dogs made no move. They waited, skittish and eager, aware that Vaggan was the enemy, wanting the wire out of the way for what was inevitable.

He clipped the last wire, holding the severed fence between him and the Dobermans. He dropped the clippers, fished his buck knife from the waders' pocket, and opened it. He held the blade upward, like a saber in his left hand, dropped the fence, and snatched up the pipe wrench in his right. The dogs stood, waiting. He studied them a moment, then stepped through the fence onto the lawn.

The male wheeled to Vaggan's left, whining eagerly, and the female took two or three steps directly backward. Then she lunged, fangs bared—a black shape catapulting at his chest. Had there been a single dog, Vaggan would have met the charge directly, to give the blow of the pipe wrench its full, killing force. But the male dog would also be coming. Vaggan wheeled to the right as he struck, taking some of the force out of the swing but putting the female's body between him and the charging male. The wrench slammed into the Doberman's skull in front of the ear, breaking jawbone, skull, and vertebrae. But the force of her lunge knocked Vaggan against the fence just as the male struck. It fastened, snarling, on the rubber leg of his waders, its weight pulling and tearing at him, jerking him off balance. Vaggan hit it across the lower back with the wrench, heard something break, and hit it again across the chest. The dog fell away from him and lay on its side on the lawn, struggled to get to its front feet, tried to crawl away from him. Vaggan walked after it and killed it with the wrench. The female, he saw, was already dead.

Vaggan knelt beside the male dog's body, eyes on Leonard's house, listening. No lights came on. The Santa Ana had faded a little for the moment, as if it were listening with him. Then it howled again, bending the eucalyptus trees that shaded the swimming pool and battering the shrubbery behind him. Vaggan walked back to the hole in the fence and looked through it, up and down the moonlit street. The wind moved everything, but he could see no sign of human life.

He dragged the male dog back to the shrubbery and hung it, head dangling, in the thick limbs. He extracted a rubber ice pack from his airline bag, unscrewed its oversized cap, and cut the Doberman's throat with the buck knife. He'd bought the ice bag at a medical supply store, choosing it because of its mouth, wide enough for ice cubes or to catch a flow of blood in the dark. He collected a pint or so from the dog's severed artery and then replaced the cap. Next he took out two plastic garbage bags and unfolded them on the grass. He decapitated both dogs and amputated the left foreleg of the male. He stuffed the bodies in one bag and the heads and foreleg in the other. That done, he stripped off his heavy gauntlets, blood-soaked now, replacing them with a pair of thin rubber surgical gloves.

He stepped out of the waders. The male dog's teeth had torn through the heavy rubber at the knee, leaving multiple rips. He checked the leg of his coveralls. It, too, was torn but his skin hadn't been punctured. He put the gauntlets, wrench, and buck knife back in the airline bag. He took out his shoes, and slipped them on, and extracted a roll of adhesive tape, a small .32 caliber pistol, four pairs of nylon restraint handcuffs, a pressure spray can of foam insulation, and, finally, a pair of plier clamps and two cattle ear tags he'd purchased at a veterinarian supply store in Encino. He arranged this assortment in his pockets and stacked the waders and the bag containing the bodies under the shrubbery. If the situation allowed he would retrieve them. If not, it wouldn't matter because he'd left no fingerprints or any way of tracing anything. But having the dogs' bodies missing would add another touch of the macabre, and Vaggan was going to make it macabre to the maximum— macabre enough to make page one of the LA *Times* and the lead item on tomorrow's newscasts.

He walked quietly across the lawn, carrying his burden. Dogs out of the way, the next step was the burglar alarm.

Vaggan knew a lot about the alarm. The second time he'd scouted the house, he'd noticed a BURGLARS BEWARE sticker the alarm company had pasted on the side-entrance window. He'd examined the sticker through his binoculars, looked up the company's name in the phone book, and spent an afternoon as a potential customer, learning how the system worked. Jay Leonard was big in Los Angeles, a television talk show host people were proud to have as a customer. As he had with the dog trainer, Vaggan implied that Leonard was a friend. He mentioned that Leonard was well pleased with his alarm system and had suggested he get one like it. The salesman had shown him the model and explained how it worked, and Vaggan had bought one, saying he'd install it himself.

He found the control box about where the salesman had said it should be put, mounted on an inside wall of the open carport near both a power source and a telephone line. It was equipped with an anti-tamper device that set off the alarm inside the house and flashed a signal to the Beverly Hills police if the power was cut off. Vaggan fished the aerosol can from his jacket pocket, shook it vigorously, and inserted the nozzle into the heat/moisture vent on the side of the metal box. He depressed the button and listened to the hiss of the foam insulation gushing in. The label specified a drying time of thirty minutes but, when Vaggan had checked it, it had been solid in eighteen minutes—solid and expanded to congeal all the alarm's relay switches and circuits into useless immobility. But he waited the full thirty minutes to be safe, leaning against the carport wall, coming down from the high he'd experienced in dealing with the dogs.

There was no reason to think about what he'd do next. That was carefully planned. Instead he thought about the Navajo Project. The message from his answering service had said simply, Call Mac. That meant call McNair, which in turn meant that something must have come unglued again. Not surprising. In Vaggan's experience, jobs that started sloppily tended to continue to screw up. But it was no skin off his ass. He didn't even know what the operation involved. Something, he guessed, to do with getting rid of witnesses. McNair was under indictment, with some of his people. McNair was fairly big, and certainly very senior, in the West Coast car-stealing business, and fairly big in cocaine too, from what Vaggan had heard. And he had Koreans, and Indians, and Filipinos, and Mexicans, and such people doing his stealing. In Vaggan's estimation, that was asking for trouble, since such people were poor stock. Some of them would surely screw up and get caught and talk. Had talked, already, to the grand jury, from what he'd heard, and would be ready to nail McNair in court. Which is what you should expect when you deal with such people. Losers. All of them, except maybe the Navajos.

Something about the Navajos appealed to Vaggan. Since he'd gotten into this business, he'd been reading about them. They, too, were survivors. It was because, he was sure, of their philosophy of staying in harmony with conditions, being in tune with whatever was coming down. That made sense. He did it himself. The people who refused to believe the missiles were coming and tried to turn it off by denying it, they would die. He'd gotten in harmony with that inevitable truth, accepted it, prepared for it. He would survive. And he'd gotten in harmony with this Santa Ana wind. It didn't bother him. In fact, he'd made it a part of his cover, like the quills on a porcupine. He listened to the wind, battering and shaking things, and smiled slightly. He glanced at his watch and pushed the tip of his little finger against the foam insulation in the vent. It was stiff. Time for the final phase. Time for the rent-a-cop.

Vaggan used his glass cutter on the window, removing a pane and reaching inside to unfasten the lock and then closing it behind him quickly, as soon as he had himself and his supplies inside, to shut out the wind sound. He stood listening, giving his eyes time to adjust to this deeper darkness. He'd made no sound himself. Vaggan could be quiet as the cats he admired. But opening the window would have changed the sound level of the storm for anyone awake inside. If that had alerted anyone it was better to know it now. So he waited, stock still, using up a full five minutes.

To his right a click, a low hum. The thermostat turning on the refrigerator motor. Vaggan smelled something astringent—a cleanser, perhaps—and coffee, and dust. Behind the purr of the refrigerator, the sound of distant music. Perhaps a radio playing, or a tape. In a bedroom somewhere. Then the sound of the Santa Ana rose again, pounding against the windows, rattling limbs across the roof, screeching at the corners. It subsided. The music was replaced by a male voice, inaudibly low, and then became music again. Vaggan strained to hear. It was "Daniel," the Elton John tune. Vaggan folded his handkerchief over the lens of his penlight, pointed it at the floor, and turned it on. His eyes had adjusted now, and the glow was adequate—illuminating a modern kitchen and reflecting into an expansive living area beyond.

Vaggan crept through the open archway, his crepe soles moving from the sibilance of the kitchen tile to the total silence of a thick gold carpet. He stopped and listened again, light off. The music was a bit louder now, coming from the hallway that led from the living area into what must be a bedroom wing. He removed the handkerchief, dropped it back into his pocket, and turned on the flash. A second hallway to the left led into what seemed to be some sort of atrium-greenhouse and beyond that into darkness. Vaggan moved down the carpeted hall of the bedroom wing. He stopped at the first door, listening with an ear pressed to a wooden panel. Hearing nothing, he turned off the flash, tried the knob, turned it slowly, eased the door open. He smelled deodorant, an air freshener, soap, bathroom aromas. A flick of the flash confirmed it. Guest bathroom. Vaggan closed the door and moved to the next one. Silence again, knob turning easily, door easing open. Vaggan aimed the flash at the floor, flicked it on. The reflected light showed him an empty bed, a neat, unused bedroom. He backed out, pausing to examine the door's locking mechanism under the light. A typical bedroom lock. In the hallway again, he noticed the music was loud enough now to make out an occasional word.

"Daniel," the voice sang, "my brother . . ."

Vaggan pressed an ear against the next door. Heard nothing. The knob wouldn't turn. He tried it again to confirm it was locked, then extracted a credit card from his wallet and knelt. The lock was new, and the tongue slid back easily without a sound. Vaggan stood and pulled the door open a half inch. He replaced the credit card, fished a section of nylon stocking from his pocket, and spent a moment adjusting the holes he'd cut into it over his eyes. He inhaled, feeling the same exhilaration he'd felt facing the dogs at the fence. Adrenaline. Strength. Power. Vaggan took the .32 from his pocket, held it briefly in his palm, then returned it to the pocket. He eased the door open and looked into a room lit by moonlight reflecting through translucent drapes.

The rent-a-cop had hung his clothing across a chair beside the bed, with his belt and holster dangling from the chairback. Easy to reach, Vaggan thought, when the guard heard the dogs or heard the alarm. A careful man. He extracted a revolver from the holster, dropped it in the pocket of his jacket. The cop was sleeping in shorts and undershirt, on his side, face to the wall, breathing lightly.

Vaggan switched on the flash and shined it on the man. He was young, maybe thirty, with curly black hair and a mustache. He slept on, snoring lightly. Vaggan extracted his .32, leaned forward, touched him.

The man jerked, stiffened.

"No sound," Vaggan said. He moved the light back so it illuminated the pistol. "No reason in the world for you to get hurt. They don't pay you enough for that."

The guard rolled on his back, eyes wide, staring at the gun barrel. The light reflected from dilated pupils.

"What?" the guard said. He said it in a

whisper, back pressed against the mattress.
"Who . . .?"

"You and I have no problem," Vaggan said.
"But I've got to talk to Leonard, so I got to tie
you up."

"What?" the guard said again.

"You make any trouble, I kill you," Vaggan
said. "Noise or trouble and you're dead. Otherwise, no harm done. You just stay tied up for a
while. Okay? I'll look in now and then, and if
you've tried to get loose, then I have to kill you.
You understand that? Do you?"

"Yes," the guard said. He stared at the pistol,
and into the light that illuminated it, and above
the light, looking for the source of Vaggan's
voice.

"On your stomach, now," Vaggan whispered.
"Wrists behind you."

Vaggan fished two sets of nylon handcuffs
from the jacket. He secured the guard's wrists
behind him, then pulled him down the bed by
his ankles. He cuffed the ankles together, one
foot on each side of the metal bedpost.

The man was shaking, and his skin was wet
with perspiration under Vaggan's hand. Vaggan
grimaced and wiped his palm against the sheet.
This one would never survive, and should never
survive. When the missiles came, he would be

one of the creeping, crawling multitude of weaklings purged from the living.

"Lift your face," Vaggan whispered. He taped the guard's mouth, winding the adhesive around and around, in quick movements. "My business will take an hour," Vaggan said. "I can tolerate no sound from this room for one hour. If I hear you moving in here, I will simply step inside and kill you. Like this." He pressed the muzzle of the pistol against the skin above the guard's ear. "One shot."

The guard breathed noisily through his nostrils, shuddering. He closed his eyes and turned his face away from the pistol. Vaggan felt an overwhelming sense of repugnance. He wiped his palm against his trouser leg.

Back in the hallway he used up another full minute listening. He could hear the guard breathing, almost gasping, through the door behind him and, from the door at the end of the hall, music. Elton John had been replaced by a feminine voice singing of betrayal and loneliness. He moved to the door and pressed his ear against it. He could hear only the song. He tried the knob. Locked. He extracted the credit card, slid it through the slit, pressed back the tongue, and eased the door a half inch open. His heart was beating hard now, his breathing quick, the sound of blood in his ears. He made sure the pistol was cocked. Then he opened the door.

This room was also lit by moonlight. It shone directly on thin, translucent drapes pulled across a wall of glass—making the drapes luminescent and illuminating a pale carpet and a huge bed. On it two people slept. Jay Leonard lay on his back, right hand dangling, left arm across his face, legs spread. He wore a pajama top, unbuttoned. The other person was a woman, much younger—a brunette curled on her side away from Leonard, the filtered moonlight giving the smooth, bare skin of her buttocks the look of ivory. Vaggan smelled perfume, human sweat, the inevitable dust of the Santa Ana, and the sweet smell of marijuana. The music ended and became the muted voice of the disc jockey, talking about dog food. The radio tuner was built into the headboard of the bed, its dial a bright yellow slit in the dimness. Vaggan wondered how anyone could sleep with a radio on.

In his pocket, he touched the sharp interlocking serrations forming the teeth of the ear tags and found the plier-clamp that would crimp them together. Outside, the Santa Ana rose again, screaming in the moonlight. Vaggan glanced at his watch. Three eighteen. He'd planned for three twenty, and he waited for three twenty.

"Leonard," Vaggan said. "Wake up. I've come to get the money."

When Vaggan got back to his van it was a little after 4 A.M. He stored the plastic garbage bag with the bodies of the dogs in the back, put away his other gear, and then let the van roll quietly back down the street before starting the engine. He ticked off all he'd done, making sure that nothing had been overlooked. After finishing with Leonard, he'd taken the dog's leg and used it and the ice bag of blood to make a crazy pattern of paw prints across the living room carpet and down the hall to Leonard's bedroom. He'd put the dogs' heads, side by side, on the mantel and poured the remainder of the blood over them. He'd called the hospital emergency room to tell them Jay Leonard, the TV talk show host, was on his way and would need attention. Finally he called the city desk of the *Times* and the night shift of the newsrooms of the three network TV stations. At each place someone was waiting for a call "about three forty-five," just as Vaggan had told them to be.

"I'm the man who called earlier," Vaggan said. "The celebrity I told you about who was going to get hurt tonight is Jay Leonard. He's on his way right now to the emergency room, just like I told you he would be. His girlfriend is driving him. He's got cattle ear tags clamped through both ears, and he'll need a little surgery to get them removed. If you sent a crew there, like I suggested, you should get some good stuff."

And then he told them the motive of this affair—a matter of not paying one's gambling debts. Leonard had been a fellow who didn't believe kneecaps still got broken, but Leonard knew better now, and Leonard was paying up in full, with interest.

Finally, Vaggan added, Leonard had left his house open and the lights on, and if they hurried and got there before the Beverly Hills police got the word, they would find something interesting.

CHEE EMERGED FROM SLEEP abruptly, as was his
way, aware first of the alien sheet against his
chin, the alien smells, the alien darkness. Then
he clicked into place. Los Angeles. A room in
Motel 6, West Hollywood. He looked at his
watch. Not quite five thirty. The sound of the
wind, which had troubled his sleep throughout
the night, had diminished now. Chee yawned
and stretched. No reason to get up. He had
come with a single lead to finding Begay and
Margaret Billy Sosi, the Gorman address. That
had led nowhere. Beyond that he had nothing
but the chance of picking up some trace of the
Gorman family or the Turkey Clan. He and
Shaw had tried the Los Angeles County Native
America Center with no luck at all. The woman
who seemed to be in charge was an Eastern
Indian, a Seminole, Chee guessed, or Cherokee,
or Choctaw, or something like that. Certainly

not a Navajo, or any of the southwestern tribes whose facial characteristics were familiar to Chee.

Nor was she particularly helpful. The notion of clans seemed strange to her, and the address of the three Navajos she finally managed to come up with had been dead ends. One was a middle-aged woman of the Standing Rock People, born for the Salt Cedars, another was a younger woman, a Many Goats and Streams Come Together Navajo, and the third, incredible as it seemed to Chee, was a young man who seemed to have no knowledge of his clan relationships. The project had taken hour after hour of fighting traffic on the freeways through the endless sprawl of Los Angeles, hunting through the evening darkness and into the night and getting nothing from it but a list of names of other Navajos who might know somebody in the diminished circle of Ashie Begay's diminished clan. Probably, Chee knew, they wouldn't.

Chee got up and took a shower with the water on low to avoid disturbing his motel neighbors. The shorts and socks he'd rinsed the night before were still damp, reminding him that even with the dry Santa Ana blowing all night there was a lot more humidity on the coast than in the high country. He sat in the clammy shorts, pulling on clinging wet socks, noticing that the light wind he had awakened to had faded into a calm. That meant the Pacific low-pressure area into which the wind had been blowing had moved inland. It would be a day of good weather, he thought, and the thought reminded him of how impressed Mary Landon had been (or pretended to be—it didn't really matter) with his grasp of weather patterns.

"Just like the stereotype," she'd said, smiling at him. "Noble Savage Understands the Elements."

"Just like common sense," Chee had told her. "Farmers and ranchers and people who work outside, like surveying crews and tribal cops, pay attention to the weather news. We watch Bill Eisenhood on Channel Four, and he tells us what the jet stream is doing and shows us the hundred-and-fifty-millibar map."

But he didn't want to think about Mary Landon. He opened the blinds and looked out into the gray dawn light. Still air. Street empty except for a black man in blue coveralls standing at a bus stop. The world of Mary Landon. A row of signs proclaiming what could be had for money stretching up the decrepit infinity of the West Hollywood street. Chee remembered what he'd seen on Sunset Boulevard last night on his Navajo hunt with Shaw. The whores waiting on the corners, huddling against the wind. Chee had seen whores before. Gallup had them, and Albuquerque's Central Avenue swarmed with them in State Fair season. But many of these were simply children. He commented on that to Shaw, surprised. Shaw had merely grunted. "Started a few years ago," he said. "Maybe as early as the late sixties. We don't try to buck it any more." This, too, was part of Mary Landon's world. Not that the Dinee had no prostitution. It went all the way back to the story of their origins in the underworld. The woman's sexuality was recognized as having monetary value in their marriage traditions. A man who had intercourse with a woman outside of wedlock was expected to pay the woman's family, and to fail to do so was akin to theft. But not children. Never children. And never anything as dismal as he'd seen last night on Sunset.

The black man at the bus stop put his hand in his rear pocket and scratched his rump. Watching, Chee became aware that his own rump was itching. He scratched, and made himself aware of his hypocrisy.

All alike under the skin, he thought, in every important way, despite my Navajo superiority. We want to eat, to sleep, to copulate and reproduce our genes, to be warm and dry and safe against tomorrow. Those are the important things, so what's my hang-up?

"What's your hang-up, Jim Chee?" Mary Landon had asked him. She had been sitting against the passenger door of his pickup, as far from him as the horizon. "What gives you the right to be so superior?" All of her was in darkness except for the little moonlight falling on her knees through the windshield.

And he had said something about not being superior, but merely making a comparison. Having a telephone is good. So is having space to move around in, and relatives around you. "But schools," she'd said. "We want our children to get good educations." And he'd said, "What's so wrong with the one where you're teaching?" and she'd said, "You know what's wrong," and he'd said . . .

Chee went for breakfast to a Denny's down the street, putting Mary Landon out of his mind by escaping into the problem presented by Margaret Sosi. This puzzle, while it defied solution, improved his appetite. He ordered beef stew.

The waitress looked tired. "You just getting off work?" she asked, jotting the order on her pad.

"Just going to work," Chee said.

She looked at him. "Beef stew for breakfast?"

Mexican, Chee thought, but from what Shaw had said she probably wasn't. Not in this part of Los Angeles. She must be a Filipino. "It's what you get used to," Chee said. "I didn't grow up on bacon and eggs. Or pancakes."

The woman's indifference vanished. "Burritos," she said. "Refritos folded in a blue corn tortilla." Smiling.

"Fried bread and mutton," Chee said, returning the grin. "Down with the Anglos and their Egg McMuffin." And so much for Shaw's generalizations about his home territory. The only people Chee had ever known who would willingly eat refried beans wrapped in a tortilla were Mexicans. Chee doubted if Filipinos would share any such culinary aberration.

He ate his stew, which had very little meat in it. Maybe this woman was the only Spanish speaker in West Hollywood who wasn't from the Philippines, but Chee doubted it. Even if she was, she represented the flaw in generalizing about people. On the Big Reservation, where people were scarce and scattered, one tended to know people as individuals and there was no reason to lump them into categories. Shaw had a different problem with the swarming masses in his jurisdiction. People in West Hollywood were Koreans or Filipinos, or some other category that could be labeled.

Just like people in old folks' homes were senile. Policemen wouldn't bother questioning senile people. Chee hurried through his stew.

▷◁

The legend on the door of the Silver Threads Rest Home declared that visiting hours were from 2 to 4 P.M. Chee glanced at his watch. It was not yet 8 A.M. He didn't bother to ring the bell. He walked back to the sidewalk and began strolling along the chain-link fence. On his third circuit, four old people had appeared on the east-facing porch, sitting in their mute and motionless row in their immobile wheelchairs. While Chee strolled, a red-faced boy wearing a white smock backed through the doorway with a fifth wheelchair in tow. It held a frail woman wearing thick-lensed glasses. Mr. Berger and his aluminum walking frame had not appeared. Chee continued his circumnavigation, turning up the alley and confirming that residents of the nursing home had a fine view of the apartments where the late Albert Gorman had lived—from the porch or from the lawn. On the next circuit, Berger appeared.

As Chee rounded the corner that brought him past the east porch, the old man was shuffling his way toward the fence, moving the walker, leaning on it, then bringing his legs along. Chee stopped at the fence at the point for which Berger was aiming. He waited, turning his back to the fence and to the old man's struggle. Behind him he could hear Berger's panting breath.

"Sons a bitches," the man was saying. Describing, Chee guessed, either the nursing home staff or his own recalcitrant legs. Chee heard Berger place the walker beside the fence and sigh and grunt as he dragged his legs under him. Only then did he turn.

"Good to see you, Mr. Berger," Chee said. "I was hoping I wouldn't have to wait for visiting hours."

"Coming to see . . ." The surprise was in the tone before Berger's tongue balked at the rest of it. His face twisted with the struggle, turning slightly red.

"I wanted to talk to you some more about Gorman," Chee said. "I remember you asked me if he was in trouble, and as a matter of fact he was in very deep trouble, so I thought maybe you had some idea of what was going on." Chee was careful not to phrase it as more than an implied question.

Mr. Berger opened his mouth slightly. Made a wry expression.

"He might have been in worse trouble than he knew. Somebody followed him from here to Shiprock. In New Mexico. On the Navajo Reservation. They shot each other, Gorman and this guy. Gorman killed the man. And then Gorman died himself."

Berger looked down at his hands, gripping the metal frame of the walker. He shook his head.

"We don't know why anyone would have wanted to kill Gorman," Chee said. "Doesn't seem to be any reason for it. Did Gorman tell you anything that would help?"

Berger's white head rose. He looked at Chee, drew a deep and careful breath, closed his eyes, concentrated.

"Man came," he said.

Chee waited.

Berger struggled, gave up. "Shit," Berger said.

"Would it help if I fill in the gaps? I'm going to guess at some of it. And if I'm wrong you shake your head and I'll stop. Or I'll try another guess."

Berger nodded.

"A man came to see Gorman, here at the apartment."

Berger nodded.

"The day before Gorman left for New Mexico?"

Berger took his hands from the walker, held them about a foot apart, moved them together.

"Less than that," Chee said. "The night before Gorman left."

Berger nodded.

"You saw him?"

Berger nodded. He pointed to Gorman's apartment. Then indicated height and breadth.

"A big man," Chee said. "Very big?"

Berger agreed.

"How old?"

Berger struggled with that. Chee held up his hands, flashed ten fingers, another ten, stopped. Berger signaled thirty, hesitated, added ten.

"Maybe forty," Chee said. "Another Navajo?"

Berger canceled that, pointing to his own hair.

"White," Chee said. "Blond?"

Berger nodded.

"A big blond man came here just before Gorman left for New Mexico," Chee said. Lerner, he was thinking, was neither big nor blond. "Had you seen him before?"

Berger had.

"Often?"

Berger held up two fingers.

"They talked?" Chee had begun wondering where this was taking him. What could Berger know that would be useful?

Berger had taken his hands from the walker. His fingers, twisted and trembling, became two men standing slightly apart. Wagging fingers indicated one man talking, then the other man talking. Then the two hands moved together, parallel, to Berger's left. He stopped them. His lips struggled with an impossible word. "Car," he said.

"They walked together to a car after talking. The blond man's car?"

Berger nodded, pleased. His hands resumed their walk, stopped. Suddenly the right hand attacked the left, snatched it, bent it. Berger looked at Chee, awaiting the question.

Chee frowned. "The blond man attacked Gorman?"

Berger denied it.

"Gorman attacked the blond man?"

Berger agreed. He struggled for words, excited.

Chee bit back a question. "Interesting," he said, smiling at Berger, giving him time. He had an idea. He tapped Berger's right hand. "This is Blond," he said, "and the left hand is Gorman. Okay?"

Berger grasped his right hand with his left, began to enact a struggle. Then he stopped, thinking. He grasped an imaginary doorknob, opened the imaginary door, watching to see if Chee was with him.

"One of them opened the car door? The blond?"

Berger agreed. He held his left hand with his right, released it, then pantomimed, fiercely, the slamming of the door. He clutched the injured finger, squirming and grimacing in mock pain.

"Gorman slammed the door on the blond man's finger," Chee said. Berger nodded. He was a dignified man, and all this play-acting was embarrassing for him. "That would suggest that Gorman wasn't going to the car willingly. Right? You were standing about here, watching?" Chee laughed. "And wondering what the hell was going on, I'll bet."

"Exactly," Berger said, clearly and distinctly. "Then Gorman ran." He motioned past the fence, up the alley, a gesture that caused Gorman to vanish.

"And the blond man?"

"Sat," Berger said. "Just a min . . ." He couldn't finish the word.

"And then I guess he drove away."

Berger nodded.

"You have any idea about all this?"

Berger nodded affirmatively. They looked at each other, stymied.

"Any luck writing?" Chee asked.

Berger held up his hands. They trembled. Berger controlled them. They trembled again.

"Well," Chee said, "we'll figure out a way."

"He came," Berger said, pointing to the gravel where Chee was standing. "Talked."

"Gorman. About the trouble he was in."

Berger tried to speak. Tried again. Hit the

walker fiercely with a palsied fist. "Shit," he said.

"What did Gorman do for a living?"

"Stole cars," Berger said.

That surprised Chee. Why would Gorman tell Berger that? But why not? A new dimension of Albert Gorman opened. One lonely man meeting another beside a fence. Berger's potential importance in this affair clicked upward. Frail, bony, pale, he leaned on the walker frame, trying to form another word, his blue eyes intense with the concentration.

Chee waited. The woman whose son was coming to see her had posted her wheelchair down the fence. Now she rolled it across the parched, hard-packed lawn toward them. She noticed Chee watching her and turned the wheelchair abruptly into the fence. "He's coming," she said to no one in particular.

"Gorman stole cars," Chee said. "And the man he stole them for—the man who paid him—got indicted by the federal grand jury. Maybe the reason he went to New Mexico, and the reason somebody followed to shoot him, was because he was going to be a witness against his boss. Maybe the boss . . ."

But Berger was denying that, shaking his head.

"You don't think so?"

Berger didn't. Emphatically.

"He talked to you about that, then?"

Berger agreed. Waved that subject off. Tried to form a word. "Not go," he managed finally. His mouth worked to say more, but couldn't. "Shit," he said.

"Not go?" Chee repeated. He didn't understand that.

Berger was still trying to find words. He couldn't. He shrugged, slumped, looked ashamed.

"He showed him a picture." The words came from the woman in the wheelchair. She was looking out through the fence, and Chee didn't realize that the statement had anything to do with Berger until he saw the old man was nodding eagerly.

"Gorman showed Mr. Berger a picture?" he asked.

"That Indian showed that fella you're talking to there a picture," the woman said. She pointed at Berger. "Like a postcard."

"Ah," Chee said. The photograph again. Why was it so important? It didn't surprise him to see the woman's senility fall away. It would come again just as quickly. Chee had grown up surrounded by the old of his family, learning from them, watching them grow wise, and ill, and die. This end of the human existence had no more mystery for him than its beginning.

"Picture," Berger said. "His brother."

"Was it a picture of an aluminum trailer with a man standing by it?"

It was.

"And Gorman said it was from his brother?"

Berger nodded again.

"I don't know what you meant when you said 'Not go.' I'm confused because we know Gorman went. Was it that Gorman had decided not to go and then changed his mind?"

Berger denied it, emphatically. He recast his palsied hands in the roles of Gorman and the blond man. The hand representing Gorman dipped its fingertip affirmatively. The hand representing the blond man shook its fingertip negatively.

"I see," Chee said. "Gorman wanted to go. The blond man said not to." He glanced at Berger, who was agreeing. "So Gorman was going, the blond man tried to stop him, they fought, and Gorman went. Good a guess as any?"

Berger shrugged, unhappy with that interpretation. He pointed to the dial of his watch.

"Time?" Chee was puzzled.

Berger tapped the dial, pointing to where the hour hand was. Then he moved his finger around the dial, counterclockwise.

"Earlier?" Chee asked.

Berger nodded.

"You mean this happened earlier? This business about Gorman wanting to go and the blond man telling him not to?"

Berger was nodding vigorously.

"Before the fight? Before the evening Gorman hurt Blond Man's hand? A day before? Two days?"

Berger was nodding through all this. Two days before was correct. "And Gorman told you about that?"

"Right," Berger said.

"Do you know why Gorman wanted to go?"

"Worried," Berger said. He tried to say more, failed, shrugged it off.

The red-faced young man Chee had noticed earlier was slouching across the lawn toward them, whistling between his teeth. The woman spun her wheelchair and hurried it down the fence away from him. "Mean old bitch," the young man said, and hurried after her.

"Do you know what was written on the postcard? The one with the picture on it?"

Berger didn't.

"The woman said it was like a postcard," Chee said. "Was it?"

Berger looked puzzled.

"Did it have a stamp on it?"

Berger thought, closed his eyes, frowning. Then he shrugged.

"She was a very observant woman," Chee said. "I wonder if either one of you happened to see a Navajo girl show up at Gorman's apartment yesterday. Little. Skinny teenager, wearing a navy pea coat. You see her?"

Berger hadn't. He looked after the woman, wheeling furiously across the grass with the red-faced man hurrying after her. "Smart," he said. "Sometimes."

"I had an aunt like that," Chee said. "Actually my mother's aunt. When she could remember she was very, very smart. Yesterday our friend couldn't remember anything."

"Excited," Berger said. He tried to explain. Failed. Stopped. Stared down at his feet. When he looked up again, he was excited. And he had a plan.

"War," he said. He held up two fingers.

Chee thought about that. "World War Two," he guessed.

"Son," Berger said. He tried to go on and failed.

"In the war," Chee said.

Berger nodded. "Navy."

"He was killed," Chee guessed.

Berger shook that off. "Big shot," he said. "Rich." That exhausted Berger's supply of words. His mouth twisted. His face turned pink. He pounded at the walker.

The red-faced young man had caught the woman's wheelchair and was pushing her toward the porch. She sat, eyes closed, face blank. So her son was rich and important, Chee thought. What was Berger trying to tell him with that. Her son had been in the navy forty years ago, now he was rich and important, and that was related to something causing her to be excited yesterday.

"Hey!" Chee shouted, suddenly understanding. "Yesterday. Yesterday morning she saw a sailor, is that it?"

Berger nodded, delighted at the breakthrough.

"Maybe she saw a sailor," Chee told Berger. "Maybe she saw Margaret Sosi in her pea jacket. What's that woman's name?"

Berger got it out the first try. "Ellis."

"Mrs. Ellis," Chee shouted. "Did you see a sailor yesterday? At the apartments?"

"I saw him," Mrs. Ellis said.

"He looked like your son. In a blue pea coat?"

"I don't have a son," Mrs. Ellis said.

> 15 <

THE MAN MCNAIR CALLED HENRY brought Vaggan his water in a crystal glass. Vaggan had said, "No ice, please," but the man named Henry hadn't listened, or hadn't cared. Henry's expression had suggested that he found bringing Vaggan a glass of water distasteful. He was a plump, soft man, with a soft voice and shrewd eyes that he allowed to give him an expression of haughty contempt. Vaggan placed the glass on the coffee table, aware of the two ice cubes floating in it but not looking at it.

"You're a day late," McNair said. "I called you yesterday morning, and I said there was a hurry for this." McNair opened a black onyx box on his desk, extracted a cigaret, and tapped it against his thumbnail. "I don't like people who work for me to be late."

Vaggan was feeling fine. He'd gotten home from the Leonard business before dawn, show-ered, done his relaxing exercises, and slept for six hours. Then he'd exercised again, weighed, and had a breakfast of wheat germ, alfalfa sprouts, and cheese while he watched the noon TV news. The NBC channel had led with Leonard being rushed through the emergency room doors and propelled away with one bloody ear visible. He switched quickly to ABC-TV and caught the tag end of his own voice, recorded from his final telephone call, explaining about the welshed debt. The Man could hardly ask more. Perfect. He'd switched off the set then and called the McNair number. He'd told the man who answered—probably Henry—to tell McNair he'd be there at 2 P.M.

It was an easy hour's drive. He killed the remaining time reading through his new copies of *Survival* and *Soldier of Fortune*. He clipped out an article on common medicinal herbs of the Pacific Coast and circled an advertisement of Freedom Arsenal offering an FN-LAR assault rifle for $1,795. He'd looked at an FN in a Pasadena sporting goods store—the same model built by Fabrique National in Belgium for NATO paratroops. He'd been impressed, but the price there had been $2,300, plus California sales tax. With the Leonard money, he could afford either price, but most of that money would have to go to the contractor to finish the concrete work on his storage bunker, and he also wanted to install a solar generator and add to his stock of ammunition. However, there'd be more money coming in from McNair. Vaggan felt fine.

He left at 1 P.M., giving himself a bit more time than he needed to drive into the Flinthills district, where the McNair family had bought itself a hill and built itself an estate and raised its offspring. And now he sat in the McNair office, or study, or library, or whatever such rooms were called in such houses, and here across the desk was McNair himself. McNair interested him. Very few men did.

"I am never late," Vaggan said. "Maybe Henry didn't tell you." He glanced over his shoulder at Henry, who was standing stiffly beside the doorway. "Henry," he said. "Come here."

Henry hesitated, looking past Vaggan at McNair. But he came.

"Here," Vaggan said. He extracted the two ice cubes from the glass and held them out to Henry. "You can have these," he said. "I said no ice."

Henry's face flushed. He took the cubes and stalked out of the room.

Vaggan took out his handkerchief and dried his fingers.

"Hard to get reliable help," he said to McNair.

McNair had understood the subtlety of the point Vaggan was making, appreciating how the threat had been made without ever being spoken. He made a wry face and nodded.

"Henry," he called.

Henry reappeared at the door.

"Bring Mr. Vaggan a glass of water, please."

"Yes, sir," Henry said.

"So what needs doing?" Vaggan said.

"More Navajo business," McNair said. He had a heavy, rawboned face, pale and marked with the liver marks common with lightly pigmented people when they age. His eyes were an odd color, something near green, sunken under heavy, bristling gray brows. His expression was sour. "More trouble from the Gorman screwup," he added. "A young woman named"— McNair looked down at a note pad on his desk—"named Margaret Sosi came to Los Angeles from Shiprock. She had a photograph of Leroy Gorman, and she came to Albert's place in West Hollywood looking for him. I want you to find her."

"Just find her," Vaggan said.

McNair grinned, more or less, showing white, even teeth. Henry had not had even teeth. It seemed to Vaggan that it was one of the few remaining signs left in America of social position versus family poverty. Rich people could afford orthodontists.

"I don't get involved with what happens after you find her. Just make sure she doesn't make any trouble." He lit the cigaret with a silver lighter extracted from the end of the onyx box. "Absolutely sure. I do not want her talking to anybody."

He exhaled a cloud of smoke.

"And I want that picture. I want it brought to me, personally. I want an end to it."

Vaggan said nothing. A map of Scotland printed on something that looked like parchment dominated the wall behind McNair. Its borders were decorated by patches of plaid which Vaggan presumed were the tartans of the Scottish clans. A bagpipe and a heavy belt holding a scabbarded sword hung beside it. A claymore, Vaggan thought. Wasn't that the Scottish name for it? Down the wall were photographs. People in kilts. People in fox-hunting coats. A photograph of Queen Elizabeth II, an autograph scrawled across the bottom.

"Here's her description," McNair said. He held out a sheet of typing paper.

"I hope you have a little more than that," Vaggan said. "If you want her found this year."

"I have an address."

"Addresses help," Vaggan said.

"If she's still there," McNair said. "It was yesterday morning when I called you."

"Maybe we'll be lucky," Vaggan said. "Anyway, it's a place to pick up the trail."

McNair was holding the typing paper, folded, between his fingers, tapping the edge of the fold against the desk, looking at Vaggan.

"How'll you do it?"

"What? Find her?"

"Kill her."

Henry had replaced the water with another crystal glass and disappeared. No ice cubes. Vaggan sipped, looking over the rim of the glass at McNair. He was thinking of tape recordings, but he could think of nothing McNair could gain by taping this conversation. Still, it was an odd question. Vaggan answered with a shrug and put down the glass. McNair interested him more and more. But the job was suddenly less appealing. Such things should be strictly business. No pleasure mixed in.

"I would have thought you'd have a favorite method," McNair said. His expression was bland, but the greenish eyes in their deep sockets were avid.

It should be purely business, Vaggan thought. Otherwise things get too complicated. Hard to calculate, which made them needlessly risky.

Did he need this job? Did he still want to work for McNair?

"If I did your work, I'd have a favorite method," McNair repeated.

Vaggan shrugged again, took another sip of the tepid tap water. Outside, the McNair lawn sloped away toward the Pacific. The glass was like green velvet.

"I can't see how you're going to get off," Vaggan said. "From what the story in the L.A. *Times* had to say, you're indicted on eleven counts, witnesses tying you into the business personally, everything neat and tidy the way it sounded. Why don't you jump bail, cash in a little of this"—he gestured around him at the room—"and make a run for it?" He sipped again. "Actually, there wouldn't have to be any actual running. Just transfer some cash to wherever and get some papers and fly away. Easy. No worry. No risk."

Vaggan had been studying McNair's face. It registered irritation, then distaste. About what Vaggan had expected.

"I'm not guilty," McNair said.

"Not until the jury convicts you," Vaggan said. "Then you are, and the judge raises the bail way up there, and it's all going to be a lot tougher and more expensive."

"I have never been convicted of anything,"

McNair said. "No McNair has ever been in prison. Never will be." He got up and stood by the window, his hand resting on a form Vaggan presumed was a sculpture cast in steel. "Besides, if you walk away from it, you can't take this along."

He seemed to mean the sculpture and what he saw from the window. Or perhaps it meant the bagpipe and being a McNair. Vaggan could appreciate this. One of the rulers. The hard men. An interesting man, Vaggan thought. He'd be dealing with the McNairs after the missiles, the tough ones. He understood the old man better again. The avidity he'd seen was as much like greed as it was cruelty. Cruelty bothered him because it seemed beside the point, a waste of emotions that seemed strange to him. But Vaggan could understand greed perfectly.

"I have a feeling you're balking," McNair said, still looking out the window. "Why else all this impertinence? All these questions? Will you take care of it for me?"

"All right," Vaggan said. He got up and took the paper from the old man's fingers, unfolded it, and read. The address was on a street he'd never heard of. He'd get it located on his map, and wait for dark, and get it over with.

JIM CHEE, WHO HAS ALWAYS CONSIDERED himself an excellent driver, drove now uneasily. The mixture of precise timing, skill, and confidence in their immortality that Los Angeles drivers brought to their freeway system moved Chee back and forth from anxious admiration to stoic resignation. But his luck had held so far, it should hold for another afternoon. He rolled his pickup truck through the endless sprawl of the city and the satellite towns that make Los Angeles County a wilderness of people. For a while he managed to keep track of just where he was in relation to where he had been, noticing direction shifts and remembering when he switched from one freeway to another. But soon it overwhelmed him. He concentrated solely on the freeway map, which Shaw had marked for him, and on not missing his turns. The land had risen a little now out of the flatness of the city basin, and there were traces of desert visible in vacant lots, which became vacant blocks, which became entire vacant hillsides, eroded and dotted with cactus and the dry, prickly brush common to land where it rarely rains. The poor side of the city. Chee examined it curiously. He no longer had a sense of where he was in relation to his motel. But there, low on the southwestern horizon, hung the sun. And eastward over those dry ridges lay the desert. And behind him, somewhere beyond the thickening smog of the city, was the cold, blue Pacific. It was enough to know.

And now just ahead of him was the exit sign Shaw had told him to watch for. He angled the truck cautiously across the freeway lanes and down the exit ramp and rolled to a stop on the parking ramp of a Savemor service station. Here tumbleweeds grew through the broken asphalt. A paunchy, middle-aged man in bib overalls leaned against the cashier's booth, eyeing him placidly. Chee spread his Los Angeles street map across the steering wheel, making sure he was in the right place. The sign said Jaripa Street, which seemed correct. Now the job was to locate Jacaranda, which intersected somewhere and led to the address that Shaw had pried, finally, from Gorman's landlady. Watching Shaw work had been impressive.

Chee recalled the interview. Two interviews, to be correct, although the first one had been brief. He had rung her doorbell, and rung, and rung until finally she had appeared, staring at him wordlessly past the barely opened door. She had re-inspected his Navajo Tribal Police credentials, still with no sign they impressed her. No, she'd said, she hadn't seen anyone like Margaret Billy Sosi. And then Chee had told her that a witness had seen the girl here.

"They lied," the woman had said, and closed the door firmly in Chee's face.

It had taken almost an hour for the dispatcher at LAPD to locate Shaw, and maybe twenty minutes later Shaw had arrived—driving up alone in an unmarked white sedan. The second interview had gone much better.

They'd done this one inside, in the woman's cluttered office-sitting room, and Chee had learned something from the way Shaw had handled it.

"This man hasn't got any business here," Shaw had said, pointing a thumb at Chee. "He's an Indian policeman. Couldn't arrest anybody in LA. I don't care what you told him. You could tell him to go to hell. But now I'm here."

Shaw fished out his identification and held it in front of the woman's face. "You and I've done business before, Mrs. Day," he said. "You called me when this guy showed up asking about Gorman, just like I told you to. I appreciate that. Now I need to find this girl, Margaret Sosi. She was here yesterday. What'd she say to you?"

Chee was trying to read Mrs. Day's expression. It was closed. Hostile. Was it fearful? Call it tense, he thought.

"Trashy people are always showing up here, ringing my doorbell." She glanced at Chee. "You can't expect me to remember them."

"I can," Shaw said. "I do expect it." He stared at her, face hard. "We're going to find the girl, and I'm going to ask her if she talked to you."

Mrs. Day said nothing.

"If she did, then I'm going to get the fire marshal's boys interested in this place of yours. Wiring. Exits. Trash removal. You familiar with the fire code for rental property?"

Mrs. Day looked stubborn.

"When we find this girl, if she's got her throat cut, like maybe she will have from what we know now, and you haven't helped us, then that makes you an accessory to murder. I don't guess we could prove it, but we can get you downtown, and book you in, and then you have to deal with the bonding company, and get a lawyer hired, and show up for the grand jury, and—"

"She was looking for Gorman," Mrs. Day said.

"We know that," Shaw said. "What did she say about him?"

"Nothing much. I told her Gorman wasn't here."

"What else—" Shaw began, but the telephone cut him off.

Mrs. Day looked at Shaw. On the wall behind her, the telephone rang again.

Shaw nodded.

Mrs. Day said hello into the mouthpiece, listened, said no, said I'll call you back. "Just a sec," she said. She reached behind her and wrote a number on a calendar mounted to the wall beside the phone. "I don't know. Maybe fifteen minutes," she said, and hung up.

"What else did she say?" Shaw continued.

"She was trying to find some old man. I don't remember his name. Her grandfather. Wanted to know if the old man had come here looking for Gorman."

"Had he?" Shaw asked.

"I never seen him if he did. Then she wanted to know if I had any other address for Gorman, and I gave her what I had and she went away."

"What did you give her?"

"Next of kin," Mrs. Day said. "I make my renters fill out a little card for me." She took a metal box from the desk, fingered through it, and handed Shaw a file card. "Gives them the idea that if they steal everything you got a way at getting back at 'em."

Shaw copied information into his notebook.

"Jacaranda Street? That right?"

Mrs. Day nodded.

"Never heard of it," Shaw said. "And the name's Bentwoman Tsossie? Could that be right?"

"What he said," Mrs. Day said. "Who knows about Indians?"

Shaw returned the card. Chee was looking at the calendar pad beside the telephone. It was divided into the thirty-one days of October, and Mrs. Day had written the telephone number of whoever had just called her in the October 23 space—which was today. October 22 was blank, as were many of the days. Others bore terse notations, accompanied by numbers. In the October 3 square, the word Gorman was written, with a number under it. A line ran from Gorman to another number in the margin. Chee recognized the second number. It was on a card in his billfold—the number of Shaw's telephone. Whose phone would the first number ring?

Now, as he sat in his pickup amid the tumbleweeds beside this rundown service station, the significance of all this began to take shape in Jim Chee's mind. The date was wrong. Too early. Days too early.

There was a pay phone booth at the sidewalk adjoining the station. Chee opened the truck door, swung his legs out, and stopped to think it through again. Mrs. Day had written Gorman's name in the October 3 box, at least a week before Shaw had recruited her as a watcher. Then she had written the number of Shaw's arson office number in the margin and linked it to Gorman's name with a line. But someone had contacted her a week before that and arranged for her to call a number relative to Gorman. Had she been watching him for someone else before she had watched his apartment for Shaw? What was the number? Chee recalled the number, as he was expected to recall it, without feeling particularly proud of the feat. Chee had been taught to remember when he emerged from infancy, and it was a skill his training as a *yataalii* had honed. He climbed out of the truck.

Chee called the arson number, hoping only to extract Shaw's home number. But the detective answered.

"It don't mean a thing to me," Shaw said. "It's a downtown telephone, judging from the prefix. Have you tried it?"

"No. I thought I'd ask you. It's after five so nobody is going to be there."

"Who knows?" Shaw said. "We'll just give a try. I'm going to put you on hold a minute and call it." The telephone clicked.

Chee waited. Through the dirty window of the telephone booth, he could see a row of rundown residences scattered down a street that was mostly weedy vacant lots. From across the hills, smoke rose white and gray. A brush fire, Chee guessed. Shaw had called this "poor boy territory," the habitat of losers, of transients and bums and other marginal people. He'd warned Chee not to expect the streets to match the street maps.

"I wish I could get off and go along," Shaw had said. "It's a good place to get lost, if you want to get lost. Or to lose something if you got something you don't want nobody to find. Including bodies. Every once in a while we get one reported from out there. They just turn up. Dumped behind the brush. Or somebody notices a foot sticking out after a mudslide, or old bones in a rotten sleeping bag."

The telephone clicked again. "Turned out to be an answering service," Shaw said. "And of course nobody knew anything about anything except the boss and he wasn't in. Sort of establishment you have to go down and show a badge to find out something. I'm going to put you on hold again and call the landlady."

The telephone booth smelled dusty. Chee pushed open the door to admit the outside air and got with that the aroma of warm asphalt. There was also the smell of smoke, the perfumed smoke of the desert burning that drifted down from the fire over the ridge. Through that, faintly and only now and then, he could detect an acrid chemical taint—the bad breath of the city. Last night's Santa Ana wind had blown the Los Angeles smog far out over the Pacific. But that was many hours ago. The city had exhaled again. Through the window of the cashier's cage, the service station attendant was watching Chee, openly curious. Chee thought about Mary Landon. About now she'd be in her little Crownpoint teacherage preparing her supper. He saw her, as he had often seen her from his favorite chair in that tiny living-dining room, working at the drainboard, hair pulled to the top of her head, slender, intent, talking as she did whatever she was doing to the vegetable she was working on.

Chee closed his eyes, rested his head against the cool metal of the telephone box, and recreated the scene and his feeling for it. Anticipation. A good meal. But not that, really. Anticipation of a good meal in good company.

Mary across from him, checking his response to whatever she had given him, caring whether he liked it, her knee against his knee. Her—

Click. "You still there?" Shaw asked and went on without waiting. "Day said that some fellow had called her on the phone and told her that if she was willing to keep an eye on Gorman's apartment and let him know anything interesting, he was going to mail her a hundred bucks, and there would be another hundred anytime she called with anything interesting."

"Like what?"

"Like any visitors. Like Gorman packing up, moving out. Anything unusual."

"Did she make any calls?"

"She said just one. The day Gorman left for Shiprock."

"You believe her?"

"No," Shaw said. "But it might be true. Far as we know, nothing else happened."

"That's true," Chee agreed.

"Call me if you locate the girl," Shaw said. He gave Chee his home telephone number.

The service station attendant, with considerable gesturing, showed Chee that if he drove directly north on Jaripa he would inevitably drive right past its junction with Jacaranda.

"Map's screwed up," he said. "Jacaranda runs up into the hills about a mile from here. Access to some jackleg housing development, but the city never put in the utilities so the whole thing went down the tube. You bought in there, you got burned."

"I'm trying to find some people at thirteen thousand two hundred and seventy-one Jacaranda," Chee said. "That sound like it would be back in there?"

"God knows," the attendant said. "They got all sorts of street names and numbers back in there. Just no house to put 'em on."

"But some people do live back there," Chee said. "That right?"

"There's some," the man said. "Beats sleeping under a bridge. But if you're sleeping under a bridge, at least somebody didn't sell it to you." He laughed and glanced at Chee to see if he enjoyed the humor.

But Chee was thinking something else. He was thinking that whoever had paid Mrs. Day to keep track of Albert Gorman almost certainly knew all about this address.

CHEE FOUND 13271 JACARANDA STREET just as the setting sun was converting the yellow-gray smog along the western horizon into oddly beautiful layers, pink-gray alternated with pale rose, making a milder, more pastel display than the garish sunsets of the high desert country. He had enjoyed the hunt. The scenery was different: desert, but low-altitude desert, and without the bitter winters of the Big Reservation it produced a different kind of vegetation. He had decided fairly early that he wouldn't find the Jacaranda address, that it was simply a number Gorman had pulled from the air to satisfy Mrs. Day's requirement. Tomorrow morning he would get up early, drive back to Shiprock, and put out feelers at St. Catherine and Two Gray Hills and here and there, to make sure he'd know if and when Margaret Sosi returned to home country. And he'd drive over to Crownpoint and talk to Mary Landon. And, having time to think about it, Mary Landon would have decided that raising their children Dinee and among the Dinee was, after all, what she really wanted to do. Or maybe not. Probably not. Almost certainly not. And what then? What would he do?

Meanwhile Chee drove. The junction of Jacaranda Drive was marked by a huge billboard that rose from a fieldstone base and was topped by the legend J C R ND EST TES in raised wooden letters, once red. Even expecting it, it took Chee a moment to recognize JACARANDA ESTATES with the A's stolen. And to wonder who had such a specialized need for letters. Below the defaced name the billboard featured a map. A great green blob in the middle was labeled Golf Course, and a dim blue oblong near the center of the green was marked Trout Lake. Other landmarks included Shopping Center, Post Office, School, and Country Club. Nothing on the map seemed to bear any relationship to the reality of lonely desert foothills around him, but Chee studied the network of streets it displayed. Jacaranda meandered east-southeast, a main artery. He felt encouraged.

The encouragement was brief. Jacaranda's asphalt surface, already cracked and weedy, gave way to gravel within a quarter mile, and the gravel that replaced it was soon replaced in turn by graded dirt, replaced by a rutted track from which streets led, streets which were nothing more than a few passes made by a bulldozer years ago. Chee passed street signs (Jelso, Jane, Jenkins, Jardin, Jellico), warped plywood boards mounted on two-by-fours with their paint weathered almost beyond the point of legibility. Jane Street had offered a half dozen dilapidated mobile homes clustered near a rusty water tank. On Jenkins he passed a concrete foundation, on Jellico an abandoned frame house from which doors and window frames had been looted. But mostly there was only emptiness. Judy, July, Jerri, and Jennifer streets offered nothing but creosote brush, sandstone, and cacti. Beyond Jennifer, the erosion of an arroyo had erased Jacaranda.

Chee detoured, and detoured again, and rediscovered Jacaranda—worse than ever. And finally, over a ridge, there were homes again—a dented aluminum mobile home on a foundation of cinder blocks and, beyond it, a frame shanty partly covered with roofing shingles, and beyond that a charred jumble of partly burned boards. In front of the mobile home, three old cars and a school bus were parked. A middle-aged man, shirtless, a blue bandanna tied around his head, had the front wheel off the bus and seemed to be replacing a brake lining. Chee stopped, rolled down his window.

"Thirteen two seventy-one Jaracanda," he shouted. "You know where it is?"

The man looked up from his work, squinted, wiped sweat from his eyebrow.

"That them Indians?" he asked. "That old woman and all?" He had a high-pitched, whining voice.

"Sounds right," Chee said. "Name's Tsossie, or something like that."

"I don't know about that," the man said. "But their place is over that ridge yonder." He gestured down the track.

Over the ridge was a house. It was a patchwork affair, apparently built by a series of owners with diminishing ambitions, money, and hope. The front section was made of neat red bricks. A subsequent builder had tried to finish it with cinder-block walls and an addition to the pitched roof, using asphalt shingles that didn't quite match the original. To this a lean-to of planks had been added, with a roof of corrugated sheet metal. The lean-to jutted from the side, and behind it was the framework skeleton of another room, roofless, floorless, and open to the wind. Judging from the collection of dead weeds the framework had accumulated, this project must have been abandoned years ago.

Beyond this house, the rusted corpses of three vehicles stood in a neat row—a delivery van, a pickup truck too cannibalized for easy identification, and a red Dodge sedan with its hood and engine missing. Beside the house, an old Chevy sedan was parked, the window of its driver's-side door held together with tape.

Chee parked on the side of the track in front of the house, tapped twice on the horn, and waited.

Almost five minutes passed. The front door opened just a little and a face peered out. A woman. Chee got out and walked slowly toward the house.

The woman at the door was old, with a round, plump face framed with graying hair. She was obviously a Navajo, and Chee introduced himself in their language—telling her his mother's clan and his father's clan and naming various aunts and uncles—both maternal and paternal—old enough or prominent enough in affairs ceremonial or political that this old woman might have heard of them.

She listened, nodded when he was finished, and motioned him inside.

"I am born to the Turkey Clan," she said. "My mother is Bentwoman Tsossie of the Turkey Clan and my father was Jefferson Tom of the Salt Dinee." She spoke in a rusty old-person's

voice, giving Chee the rest of her clan genealogy, mentioning relatives and clan connections,
a litany of names of her extended family and its
ancestors. Chee recognized a few of them: a
woman who had served long before he was
born on the Tribal Council, a singer of the
Mountain Way Chant whom his own father had
sometimes mentioned, and a man who had
been, long, long ago, a tribal judge. When she
had finished all the formalities and offered him
a bottle of cold Pepsi-Cola, Chee accepted it, and
sipped from it, and allowed the proper amount
of time to pass, and then put the bottle on the
floor beside his chair.

"My grandmother," he said, "I come here
from Shiprock in the hope that I can find a
woman of your clan. She calls herself Margaret
Billy Sosi." Chee paused. "I hope you can help
me find her."

"The girl isn't here," Bentwoman's Daughter
said. "Why do you wish to see her?"

"I work for the Dinee," Chee said. "I am a
member of the Navajo Tribal Police. We hope to
find a man of the Turkey Clan who is called
Hosteen Ashie Begay. He is the grandfather of
Margaret Billy Sosi. She is hunting for him too."
Chee paused, noticing the expression on the old
woman's face. It was skeptical. He would not
look to her like a Navajo Tribal Policeman—out

of uniform, in a travel-rumpled plaid shirt and blue jeans. Chee had the usual Navajo's propensity for personal cleanliness, plus a little more. But his only packing for this journey had been to stick his toothbrush holder in his shirt pocket and a spare pair of socks and shorts in the glove box of his pickup. Now he looked like he'd spent two nights in jail. He extracted from his hip pocket and displayed his police credentials.

The expression of Bentwoman's Daughter did not change. Perhaps, Chee thought belatedly, her skepticism was not of Chee, the rumpled stranger, but of Chee, the Navajo Policeman. The relationship between the Dinee and their police force was no more universally serene than in any other society.

"You should talk to Bentwoman," the old woman said.

Chee said nothing. Bentwoman? When he'd seen the age of Bentwoman's Daughter, he'd presumed that Bentwoman would be dead. Chee was not good at guessing age, particularly of women. But she must be eighty. Perhaps older.

Bentwoman's Daughter was waiting, her wrinkled hands folded motionless in the folds of her voluminous skirt.

"If she will talk to me," Chee said. "Yes. That would be good."

"I will see," said Bentwoman's Daughter. She raised herself painfully from her chair and hobbled past the heavy blanket that hung over the doorway leading to the rear of the house.

Chee examined the room. The blanket was a black-and-gray design popular among weavers of the Coyote Canyon area and looked very old. The only furniture was the worn overstuffed sofa where the old woman had put him, a rocking chair, and a plastic-topped dinette table. A calendar hung on the wall opposite him—a color print of the gold of autumn cottonwoods in Canyon de Chelly issued by a Flagstaff funeral home. The calendar page was August, and seven years old. Two cases of Pepsi-Cola bottles were stacked against the wall and, beside them, three five-gallon jerricans that Chee guessed held water. A kerosene lamp, its glass chimney smudged with soot, stood on the table. Obviously, such amenities as water, gaslines, electricity, and telephone service had not yet been provided by whoever had sold this addition.

Chee heard the voice of Bentwoman's Daughter, loud and patient, explaining the visitor to someone who apparently was deaf, saying that he wanted to see "Ashie Begay's granddaughter." So she's been here, Chee thought. Almost certainly, she's been here. And then the blanket curtain pushed aside and a wheelchair emerged.

The woman in the chair was blind. Chee saw that instantly. Her eyes were open, aimed past him at the front door, but they had the clouded look of the glaucoma that takes such a heavy toll among the old of his people. Blind, and partially deaf, and immensely old. Her hair was a cloud of fluffy white, and her face, toothless, had collapsed upon itself into a mass of wrinkles. This was Bentwoman.

Chee stood and introduced himself again, talking slowly and very loud, and making sure he followed all of the traditional courtesies his mother had taught him. With that out of the way, he paused a moment for a response. None came.

"Do I speak clearly enough, my grandmother?" he asked. The old woman nodded, a barely perceptible motion.

"I will tell you then why I have come here," Chee said. He started at the beginning, with going to the hogan of Ashie Begay, and what he found there, and of meeting Margaret Billy Sosi there later, and what Margaret had told him, and what he had forgotten to ask her. Finally he was finished.

Bentwoman was motionless. She's gone to sleep, Chee thought. This is going to take time.

Bentwoman's Daughter stood behind the chair, holding its handles. She sighed.

"The girl must go home," Bentwoman said in Navajo. Her voice was slow and faint. "There is nothing for her here but trouble. She must go back to her family and live among them. She must live in Dinetah."

"I will take her back to her people," Chee said. "Can you help me find her?"

"Stay here," Bentwoman said. "She will come."

Chee glanced at Bentwoman's Daughter, inquiring.

"She took the bus," Bentwoman's Daughter said. "She went into the city when the sun came up. She said she would be back before it gets dark."

"It's getting dark now," Chee said. He was conscious of how elusive Margaret Sosi had been. Something was making him uneasy. The number written on Mrs. Day's calendar hung in his mind.

"Has anyone else been here looking for the girl?" Chee said. "Asking about her?"

Bentwoman's Daughter shook her head.

"When do you think she'll be back?"

"The bus comes every hour," Bentwoman said. "It stops down there where the map is. Every hour until midnight."

"About when does it stop?"

"Twenty minutes after the hour," Bent-woman's Daughter said. "When it's on time."

Chee glanced at his watch. It was five thirty-five. Two and a half miles to the bus stop, he guessed. She might be home in fifteen or twenty minutes. If she walked fast. If the bus was on time. If—

Bentwoman made a noise in her throat. "She should go home to her family," Bentwoman said. "She wants to find Ashie Begay, my grandson. Ashie Begay is dead."

It was an unequivocal statement. A fact stated without emotion.

Bentwoman's Daughter sighed again. She looked at Chee. "He was my nephew," she explained.

"Ashie Begay is dead?" Chee asked.

"He is dead," Bentwoman said.

"Did Margaret Sosi tell you this?"

"The girl thinks he is still alive," Bentwoman said. "I told her, but she believes what she wants to believe. The young sometimes do that."

Chee opened his mouth. Closed it. How should he frame the question?

"When I was young, I too believed what I wanted to believe. But you learn," the old woman said.

"Grandmother," Chee said. "How did you learn that Ashie Begay is dead?"

"From what you told me," Bentwoman said. "And from what the girl told me."

"I thought he might be alive," Chee said. "The girl is sure he is alive."

Bentwoman's eyes were closed now. She was asleep, Chee thought. Or dead. If she was breathing under those layers of blankets and shawls, Chee could see no trace of it. But apparently Bentwoman was simply mustering her strength for what she had to tell him.

"Ashie Begay has Tewa blood in him," Bentwoman said. "His grandmother was from Jemez. The Salt Clan went out toward the morning sun, beyond the Turquoise Mountain, to get some sheep one winter, and they came back with some children from Jemez. Some of them they sold back for corn and horses, but Ashie Begay's grandmother became the wife of one of the men in the Salt Clan and bore the child who was Ashie Begay's mother. So Ashie Begay has the blood in him of the People Who Call the Clouds. Tewa blood, and Salt Clan blood, and his father married into the Turkey Clan, and his mother's lineage was Standing Rock on her father's side. And all that has to be considered when you understand why I know Ashie Begay is dead."

Bentwoman paused, to catch her breath—
which was laboring by now—or perhaps to
allow Chee to comment. Chee had no comment
to make. He didn't understand why Ashie Begay
had to be dead. None of this had helped.

Bentwoman inhaled a labored breath, stirring her layers of coverings. She began explaining Ashie Begay's lineage in terms of the
character of ancestors. Bentwoman's Daughter
stood patiently behind the wheelchair, thinking
her thoughts. Chee glanced at his watch. If the
bus was on time, if Margaret Sosi had been on
it, if she had walked rapidly, she should be
within half a mile of here by now.

"So you see," Bentwoman was saying, "Ashie
Begay, my grandson, has my blood in him too.
All this blood combines, and it makes a certain
kind of man. It makes the kind of man who
would not have allowed the Gorman boy to die
in his hogan. He would have been prudent. The
Tewas are prudent. The Salt Clan is a prudent
clan. He would have taken the Gorman boy out
of the hogan so he could die in the safe, clean
air. So the hogan would not be ruined by the
chindi."

It had taken Bentwoman a long time to say all
of this, with many pauses. Now she was silent,
breathing heavily.

"But the hogan was broken," Chee said. "The

smoke hole was closed. The north wall was broken open. Everything in it was gone."

"Was everything gone?" Bentwoman asked. "Nothing was left?"

"Nothing but trash," Chee said.

"Did you look?" Bentwoman asked.

"It was a *chindi* hogan," Chee said. "I did not go inside."

Bentwoman breathed. She coughed. She exhaled a long breath. She turned her blind eyes toward Chee, as if she could see him. "So only a *belacani* looked?"

"Yes," Chee said. "A white policeman." He knew what Bentwoman was suggesting.

She sat for a long time, her eyes closed again. Chee was aware of the changing light outside the window. The sky turning red with sunset. Darkness gathering. Margaret Sosi would be walking through that darkness. He remembered the telephone number on Mrs. Day's calendar. He wanted urgently to go and meet Margaret. He would ask her immediately what was said on that postcard. He would take no more chances.

"If Ashie Begay is alive," Bentwoman said, "one day I will hear it. Someone in the family will know and the word will come to me. If he is dead, it would not matter. But it matters because this child believes he is alive, and she will always look for him." Bentwoman paused again, catching her breath, turning her face toward Chee again. "She should be looking for other things. Not for a dead man."

"Yes," Chee said. "Grandmother, you are right."

"You think Ashie Begay is alive?"

"I don't know," Chee said. "Maybe not."

"If someone killed him, would it have been one of the People? Or would it have been a *belacani?*"

"A white man," Chee said. "I think it would have been a white man."

"Then a white man buried Albert Gorman. And a white man broke the hogan?"

"Yes," Chee said. "If Ashie Begay is dead, that must have been what happened."

"I don't think a *belacani* would know how to do it right," Bentwoman said.

"No," Chee said. He was thinking of Albert Gorman's unwashed hair.

"Somebody should find out for sure," Bentwoman said. "They should do that so this child can know her grandfather is dead. So this child can finally rest."

"Yes," Chee said. And who else would there be to do that but Jim Chee. And doing it meant going into the ghost hogan, climbing through the black hole in the north wall. It meant stepping through the doorway into darkness.

Bentwoman was facing him, awaiting his answer. Chee swallowed. "Grandmother," he said, "I will go and do what I can do."

> **18** <

CHEE DROVE SLOWLY through a darkening landscape under a glowing copper-colored sky. He
was something of a connoisseur of sunsets, a
collector of memories of gaudy cloudscapes
and glowing western horizons that the Colorado Plateau produces in remarkable season-
changing variety. But Chee had never seen a
sunset like this one—with the slanting evening
light filtering through an atmosphere of ocean-
side humidity and chemical fumes. It gave a
golden tint to objects that should be gray or tan
or even blue; and made the cool evening seem
warmer than it was, and caused Jim Chee to feel
somehow that he was in a strange land, and that
the bird call he was hearing from somewhere to
his right was not produced by a bird at all but
by something unknown, and that when he
topped the ridge he would not look down upon
the billboards proclaiming the entrance to Jacaranda Estates but upon God knows what.

At the top of the ridge, Chee pulled his pickup off the track and turned off the engine. A small figure was walking up the slope toward him. He took his binoculars from the glove box and focused them on the walker. It was Margaret Billy Sosi, as he'd guessed, looking tired. Down the slope far below a car moved along the asphalt, its lights on. Through his open window he could hear the muted roar of freeway traffic somewhere beyond the next hill. Another vehicle, driving with its parking lights, slowed to a stop past the Jacaranda entrance billboard, backed, and turned onto the development road. Chee watched it a moment, then switched back to the girl. She'd left her pea jacket somewhere and was wearing jeans and a white shirt. She was even smaller than he'd remembered. And thinner. Would she be willing to come back to the reservation with him? Maybe not. Bentwoman would help if he needed help. But first he would get the answers to the questions he had failed to ask at Begay's hogan. He would get the answer to that mean little puzzle.

The vehicle coming up the dirt track was a van, dark brown or maybe dark green. Its lights came on, illuminating the girl with backlighting. She moved off the track. The van drew even with her and stopped. The driver leaned out the window, talking to Margaret. Then the door opened, and the man stepped out. A big man, blond, maybe six-two or -three and bulky. He towered over Margaret, showing her something in his hand. Through the binoculars, the object seemed to be a wallet. Chee sucked in his breath. The big man's other hand, dangling stiffly by his side, was marked by something white. One finger was bandaged.

Chee put down the binoculars, remembering Mr. Berger's pantomimed account of the blond man who had come for Albert Gorman and had his finger slammed in the car door. He also thought of his own pistol, locked in a drawer beside his bed in Shiprock. He turned on the ignition and started the pickup rolling down the hill.

> 19 <

VAGGAN HAD NOTICED the pickup truck parked on the ridge almost the moment he'd turned on the cracked asphalt at the entrance of Jacaranda Street. It registered in his attention merely as a nuisance. If it was occupied, the occupant would be a witness. That would affect, necessarily, the way Vaggan conducted his business. The immediate business was determining if the female figure trudging up the hill in the direction of the pickup truck was Margaret Billy Sosi, as Vaggan suspected. If it was, it was good luck. Much better to pick her up here than at whatever residence he'd find at that address McNair had given him. Here it should be simple enough to get the woman in the van and to do it without arousing any alarm. Thus Vaggan had been conscious of the pickup, but only as a minor irritant. Now, suddenly, the truck engine had started and it was rolling down the hill toward him.

Vaggan had stopped the van so that when he leaned out of its driver-side window he was just behind the woman. He had said "Miss Sosi" in a clear, emphatic voice. She had stopped and turned, and stood staring at him doubtfully.

"I'm Officer Davis, Los Angeles County Sheriff's Office," Vaggan had said, holding out the leather folder of credentials he used when the situation called for him to be police. "I need to talk to you."

"What about?" Margaret Billy had asked. "Is it about my grandfather?"

"Yes," Vaggan had said, and, sure now that she'd stand there and wait for him, he opened the van door and stepped toward her. "It's about your grandfather. I need to take you to him."

Vaggan had held out the identification folder again and, as she looked at it, taken her forearm in his hand. It was a skinny arm—a bone—and Vaggan's confidence that this girl would be no problem at all was reinforced. The girl made no attempt to pull away.

"Where is he?" she asked, looking into Vaggan's eyes. "Is he all right?"

"At the hospital," Vaggan said. "Come along." It was then that Vaggan heard the truck, its motor racing suddenly, bumping erratically down the hill. It ran off the rutted track, bumping across a hummock of cactus, and then jolted back onto the road, rolling directly for them.

"Crazy son of a bitch!" Vaggan shouted. He jumped toward the van door, then jumped back. There wouldn't be time to move it. He pulled the girl away from it.

"What's wrong with him?" she said.

Vaggan didn't respond. He'd reached under his jacket, extracted his pistol, cocked it, and held it against his back.

The pickup engine died as suddenly as it had started. It ran off the road again and slid to a stop, the door opening while it was still rolling. A man was leaning out the door, and as he leaned his hat fell off.

"*Ya-tah-hey!*" the man shouted. He half fell out the door, straightened himself, and retrieved his hat. "*Ya-tah-hey!*" he shouted again.

"I think he's drunk," the woman said.

"Yes," Vaggan said. Some of the tension left him. The man reset his hat, a worn felt cowboy job, and said something to Vaggan. The man was smiling broadly, and the words were Navajo. He stopped, laughed, and repeated them.

"What'd he say?" Vaggan asked. He kept his eyes on the drunk. The man was youngish, early thirties, Vaggan guessed, and slightly stooped. His shirttail was out on one side and one of the legs of his jeans was caught in the top of a dusty boot. A streak of spittle had run down from the corner of his mouth.

The woman said nothing for a moment. She was staring at Vaggan, her expression strange. Then she said, "He said he's having trouble with his truck. It won't drive straight. He wants you to help him with it."

"Tell him to screw off," Vaggan said. He slipped the pistol back under his belt, suddenly aware he had a headache. He hadn't gotten his sleep out. Last night had been exciting. It would take him hours to unwind.

Vaggan had studied his Greater Los Angeles street map after he left McNair. Jacaranda Drive was nowhere on it. It had taken, finally, a call to the Los Angeles County Road Maintenance Department to pin down its location. Vaggan's policy was to arrive at a scene where he expected to engage in any sort of action just at dusk—when it was still light enough to see, if you knew what you were looking for, but dim enough so that witnesses would be doubtful about what they'd witnessed. Under some circumstances he would have made a preliminary trip to the site, looked it over, learned the ground. This time he located the street, but when he realized its isolation he stayed away and waited for evening. He wanted no one in

Jacaranda Drive remembering that they'd seen the van twice, the first time in clear daylight.

Vaggan had tuned in the all-news station, carried the radio outside, and put it on the concrete retaining wall beside his second cup of coffee. Like everything Vaggan owned which required power, the radio was battery-operated. In the future as Vaggan anticipated it, the radio battery would have to last only about three weeks after THE DAY. Broadcasting would be restored within hours after the bombs—and the devastating electrical surge of the nuclear explosions—had erased civilization's grid of electrical power. The emergency generators would take over, and the frequencies would be babbling with panic: civil defense orders and, mostly, cries for help. Vaggan estimated that phase would last several weeks and then die away, and there would be no more use for his radio receiver. For that brief but important period, Vaggan kept four silicon radio batteries in a little box in his freezer. More than enough.

The local news led with an account of Vaggan's operation. Vaggan sipped his coffee and listened.

"Police report a bizarre crime in Beverly Hills—with TV talk show host Jay Leonard maimed by an intruder who broke into his palatial home and drove staples through his ears.

"Police say the intruder called local newspapers and television stations after the attack to tell them that Leonard was being taken to the emergency room at Beverly Hills General. Leonard was reported in good condition at the hospital but was not available for comment. Here's what Detective Lieutenant Allen Bizett of the LAPD had to say."

Bizett said very little, reporting in a gravelly voice that Leonard said he didn't know the motive of the attack, that he had received an anonymous telephone threat, and that he had hired a guard to protect him. Bizett said the guard had been overcome by the intruder, who had also killed two guard dogs. He described the suspect as a "large Caucasian male."

With that subject exhausted, the announcer skipped to the continued hunt for an armed robber who had killed a customer and wounded a clerk in a convenience store robbery the day before, and from that to the record-breaking traffic snarl on the San Diego Freeway caused by a two-truck accident. The item had been brief, but it had been enough, and it would be bigger for both the afternoon papers and the evening TV shows. They'd have the dogs' head business, with the bodies missing, and more of the odd stuff he'd worked in, and his telephone calls, and that would give them the motive.

Enough to earn him his bonus, but he'd never had any doubt of earning that.

He finished the coffee, considered having another cup, rejected the idea. Coffee was his only deviation from his father's rule. He'd slipped into the habit his first year at West Point and rationalized its use as a stimulant his nervous system needed. Even so, even now, twenty years since the Commander had last spoken to him, he drank with a sense of uneasiness he'd never quite defined. "Weakness," the Commander had said, sitting across the breakfast table. "People make being a child an excuse for it. But it's no excuse. In Sparta they started their males at the age of eight. Took 'em away from the women. Enduring the pain. Enduring the cold. Enduring hunger. Weeding out the weakness. We encourage weakness." Vaggan could see it clearly. His father in his perfect whites, his bristling blond hair, his trim mustache, his row of ribbons. His blue eyes staring at Vaggan, proud of Vaggan, teaching Vaggan to be strong. The thought led Vaggan, as it almost always did, into ground he didn't want to enter: to West Point, and being caught, and to Roser, Cadet Captain Roser. Vaggan considered it again— just a glance at the memory for something that might have been overlooked. No. Nothing changed. The decision was correct: to kill Roser quickly, before he could make any report. The tactic had been proper. The blow with the softball bat should have been both lethal and untraceable. But somehow Roser hadn't died. Expulsion hadn't really mattered. The Point had been a disappointment, with its endless homilies about the old, dead verities which were no longer verities—if they ever had been. But the report had gone to the Commander. And the Commander had sent the telegram.

I HAVE BURIED YOU BESIDE THE WOMAN.

Vaggan hadn't known the woman. She had borne him. She must have given him the genes that accounted for his size, because the Commander was a small man. But even his earliest memories did not include her. The Commander had never mentioned her. Asking the Commander was unthinkable.

The newscaster was talking about Berlin, a subject that always caught Vaggan's attention. The Commander had believed it would begin over Berlin and Vaggan never doubted it. But this item was inconsequential—a vote of confidence in the Bundestag. And so was the rest of the newscast. The avalanche would not begin today. And so he had finished his coffee, and made a quick check of his hillside and the redoubt he was building into it, and—when the time was right—had left to find Jacaranda Drive, and now he was facing this drunken Indian who was grinning at him foolishly and ignoring his order to leave.

"Beat it," Vaggan repeated. "Or you're spending the night in the tank."

The Indian said something in Navajo and laughed. He walked around Vaggan's van, opened the passenger side door, and climbed in.

"Son of a bitch," Vaggan snarled. He would have to deal with the Indian the hard way, apparently, which would take time and maybe even attract attention. But with any luck he could pull him out by the feet, whack him, and be done with it and gone with the girl with no problems. It was almost dark, and that would help. He rushed around the van, jerking the pistol from under his belt.

He saw what was coming far too late to avoid it. A split-second awareness of the Indian launched out of the van door, the flashlight swinging, and then the burst of pain. He had time only for reflex action. His reflexes were fine, but they only flinched him away from the full force of the blow. The flashlight—four D batteries in a heavy Bakelite tube—smashed against his upper jaw, staggered him away from the door, slammed him into the side of the van.

The shock of the blow blinded him for a moment, caused him to lose awareness. Then he was on the ground, the Indian atop him. Vaggan reacted with explosive violence before the Indian could hit him again. He grabbed the man's elbow, jerked, twisted his body. The blow missed.

After that it was no contest. Vaggan weighed himself every morning just before he began his routine of pre-breakfast exercises. That morning he had weighed 225 pounds—three pounds off the weight he considered his standard. All of it was bone, muscle, and gristle, conditioned and disciplined by a regimen the Commander had started him on before he could remember. In fact, his very first memory of this part of his life was the time he had cried. He had been doing leg lifts, the Commander standing over him, the Commander's voice chanting, "Again, again, again, again . . ." and the pain of the straining muscles had come through the haze of his fatigue and started his tear ducts flowing. He hadn't been able to control it, and the Commander had noticed, and it had been an experience of searing shame. "It doesn't help you if it doesn't hurt you," the Commander always said. The pain of that experience had taught him to control his tears. Vaggan had never cried again.

Now he made no sound at all. The Indian was

quick. The Indian was strong for his size. The Indian definitely was not drunk. That illusion had vanished from Vaggan's mind with the pain of the blow. But the Indian was younger than Vaggan, and fifty pounds lighter, and without Vaggan's skills at this sort of business. It took only a matter of seconds—a brief flurry of struggle—and the Indian was pinned under him. Vaggan could feel the flashlight against his knee. He'd dropped his pistol somewhere, so he'd use the light. He slammed the heel of his hand against the side of the Indian's head, twice, stunning the man. Then he snatched the light, raised it and struck.

"Drop it," the voice said. Margaret Billy Sosi was standing just behind him, his pistol held in both hands, pointed at his head. Vaggan let the flashlight drop on the Indian's chest.

"Get off of him," the girl ordered. Instantly Vaggan was studying her. Would she shoot him? Probably not. He could get the gun from her, but it would take a little time. Vaggan rose. He touched a fingertip to the cheekbone where the blow of the flashlight had broken the skin. "He hit me," Vaggan said. He held out his hand. "Here," he said. "Give me the pistol before you shoot somebody."

The girl took two steps backward, keeping the

pistol aimed at his stomach. "He told me who you are," she said. "You're no policeman."

"Yes I am," Vaggan said. "And if you—"

"Pick him up," she said, not taking her eyes off Vaggan's face. "Put him in your truck. We've got to get him to a hospital."

"First," Vaggan said. "I've got to have my gun back." He took a step toward her.

"I'll kill you," she said.

"No you won't," Vaggan said. He laughed and took another step toward her, hand reaching.

The shot burned past his face and struck the side of the van with a thumping sound almost as loud as the muzzle blast.

Vaggan stopped, hands held open, chest high.

"The next one hits you," the girl said. "Put him in your truck."

Vaggan stopped, and slid one arm under the Indian's shoulders and the other under his knees, and lifted him gently into the passenger's side seat. The girl slid in behind him, the pistol held carefully, and they drove away.

> **20** <

CHEE HAD BEEN AWAKE perhaps forty-five minutes when he heard the voice of Shaw loud in the corridor. He'd had plenty of time to attract a nurse's aide. The girl had been willing to make a call to Shaw's office and leave word about where Chee was and to tell Shaw the hospital he was in. But Chee hadn't felt up to explaining exactly why he was in it, or how. The why was clear enough. His head was bandaged, and under the protection he could feel a great sore knot over his left eye, and a throbbing pain about at the hinge point of his jaw on the opposite side, and a persistent internal ache. Aside from that, his left hip hurt—the burning sensation of a bruised abrasion—and his nose was swollen. When he had tried to remember exactly how each of these misfortunes had occurred he found, at first, a total alarming blank. But then he recalled that injured persons, especially those suffering head injuries, often go through a brief period of amnesia. A doctor at Flagstaff had explained it to him in typical medical fashion once. "We don't understand it, but we know it doesn't last long." And gradually the details became willing to be remembered if he tried. But he didn't try much, because the headache was spectacular. Obviously the big blond man had clobbered him. That was enough to know for the moment.

Earlier, when he had first awakened, Chee had tried to get up. That mistake had touched off explosive pain behind his forehead and waves of nausea—enough to convince him that he was in no shape to do anything even if he could remember what he should be doing. So he had sent word to Shaw, and now Shaw was beside his bed, looking down at him, eyes curious.

"You found her," Shaw said. "What'd you find out?"

"What?" Chee asked. Everything seemed sort of foggy.

"The Sosi girl. The one who brought you here," Shaw said. "Who was the man with her? What'd she tell you?"

Chee began framing questions. It made his head hurt. "Just tell me about it," he said. "This end of it. How did I get here?"

Shaw pulled back the curtain screening off

the adjoining bed, confirming it was empty. He sat. "From what I can find out so far, a vehicle arrived at the emergency entrance a little after eight last night." Shaw paused, extracted a notebook from his coat pocket, and checked it. "Eight ten, you were admitted. Admitted by a girl, late teens. Thin. Dark. Probably Indian or Oriental. Large blond man driving the vehicle. He drove away while the girl was admitting you. The girl signed the admission papers as Margaret Billy Sosi." Shaw restored the notebook to his pocket. "What'd you find out?" he asked. "And how're you feeling?"

"Wonderful," Chee said. "And nothing."

He told Shaw what had happened, up to the point of hitting the blond man with the flashlight. After that it was misty.

Shaw had listened without a word, face blank, eyes on Chee's eyes.

"Describe the van," he said.

Chee described it.

"You saw the gun. No doubt about it?"

"None. And he had an arsenal in the back of the van. I just had time for a glance, but he had a rack of weapons. Automatic rifles, maybe two different kinds, shotgun, long-barreled sniper rifle with a telescopic sight, other stuff."

"Well," Shaw said. "That's interesting."

"And a metal cabinet. God knows what was in that."

"And the girl thought he was a policeman?"

Chee nodded. And wished he hadn't. His head throbbed.

Shaw took a huge breath, exhaled it. "Well, hell," he said. "You got any notions?"

"I've got a headache," Chee said.

"I'll make a phone call," Shaw said, getting up. "Get somebody to that Jacaranda address and see if we can pick up Sosi." He glanced back from the doorway. "Too bad you didn't hit him harder."

Chee didn't comment on that. Through the general haziness, he was becoming aware of what the girl had done. She'd gotten the big man to bring him to the hospital. How the hell had she managed that? He had given up looking for an answer when Shaw returned.

"Okay," he said. "They'll find her."

"I doubt it."

"Whatever," Shaw said. He stared down, peered at Chee. Made a quizzical face. "What's going on here? Have you figured it out?"

"No," Chee said.

"I know the man in the van," Shaw said. "Eric Vaggan. That guy I told you about who works for McNair. Or he has, now and then. And for other people, I guess. Sort of an enforcer."

Chee didn't say anything. He was wishing Shaw would go away.

"The girl has something to do with the McNair business," Shaw said. "No other reason for any of this. Why else would Vaggan be out there looking for her?" He waited for Chee to tell him.

"Why don't you pick up this guy? Ask him?" Chee said.

"We don't know him all that well," Shaw said. "Don't have a file on him to amount to anything. No address. Just some stuff off some telephone taps from the other end of the call. Things like that. Witnesses describing a guy who looks like that, and so forth. Nothing concrete. You said he was taking her in?"

"She said he said he was a cop."

"Had to be a reason for it. What could it be?" Chee closed his eyes. It didn't help much.

"What we need to do," Shaw said slowly, "is go see Farmer about this."

"Farmer?"

"The Assistant U.S.D.A. The man handling the McNair case. Maybe it fits something he knows. When can you get out of here?"

"I don't know," Chee said.

"I'll handle it, then," Shaw said. "I'll do it right now."

▷◁

It was late afternoon when Shaw called. A nurse's aide had brought Chee his lunch, and a doctor had come in and removed the bandage and inspected him, and said something about not trying to knock down walls with his head. This had caused the nurse attending to chuckle. Chee had asked when he could check out, and the doctor had said he was suffering from concussion and should stay another day to see how things went. They seemed to be going well, physically. He felt better after the meal; his vision was no longer blurred, and the headache had become both intermittent and tolerable. When the woman came up from the business office to talk to him about who was going to pay for all this, he found his memory had regained full Chee-like efficiency. He rattled off the name of his Tribal Police medical insurance company, the amount of the deductible, and even the eight digits of his account number. By the time the telephone beside his bed rang, the only thing bothering him much was the scraped bruise on his hip.

Shaw hadn't had much luck.

"Typical," he said. "Farmer's long gone. He quit the Justice Department and went to work with some law firm up in San Francisco. The man who has the case now apparently hasn't even read the file on it."

The noise Chee made must have sounded incredulous.

"What's the hurry?" Shaw said, sounding a little bitter. "McNair doesn't come to trial for a couple of months, and then there'll probably be an extension. So I sit there in his office cooling my heels while he reads through the file, and then he looks up and says, 'Okay, now, what was it you want?' Like I was asking him some damn favor."

Chee made a sympathetic sound.

"So I tell him all about the business with Margaret Sosi, and so forth, and he listens politely and gets rid of me."

"Did you tell him about the Leroy Gorman angle, and Grayson, and the trailer?"

"I mentioned it," Shaw said. "Yes."

"What'd he say."

"He opened the file again, and looked through it, and then he changed the subject."

"What'd ya think?"

"Well," Shaw said, slowly, "I think that Grayson showed up in his file as one of his protected witnesses. Namely, Leroy Gorman."

"Yeah," Chee said. "I don't see how it could be any other way."

"Wasted time," Shaw said. "Wasted time. We

could already guess that." There was silence on the telephone while Shaw considered this. He sighed. "Ah, well," he said. "I don't guess that lawyer was as dumb as he acted. At least he's alerted now that they're after Gorman. Either he'll move him someplace safer or watch him."

Chee didn't comment on that. He hadn't had enough experience with Assistant U.S. District Attorneys to judge.

"What I think I'll do now is try to get a line on this Vaggan. I'd like to find out where he lives and pick him up on something. I'll get you to sign a complaint. Pick him up and see if I can learn something. What are you going to do?"

"I guess I'm going to keep trying to find Margaret Sosi. Unless you found her?"

"No," Shaw said. "She'd got back to that place on Jacaranda and got her stuff and took off. At least that's what the old woman out there said. And she wasn't around." Shaw paused. "Where you going to look for her now?"

Chee's head was aching again.

"It takes too long to explain," he said.

> 21 <

HE CALLED MARY LANDON that afternoon and told her what had happened to him, and that he'd come home as soon as they'd let him out of the hospital, which would probably be tomorrow. And when he'd finished the conversation he felt much better. Mary had been suitably upset: alarmed at first, then angry that he'd let it happen, then concerned. She'd take time off from school and come right out. No, he'd told her. By the time she got to Los Angeles, he'd probably be on his way back to Shiprock. She'd come anyway. Don't, he told her. Far too much hassle and there'd be nothing she could do. And then they'd talked of other things, never allowing the talk to drift anywhere near the central core of their problem. It was like their old warm, happy times, and when the nurse came in and Chee said he had to hang up, Mary Landon said, "I love you, Jim," and Chee, conscious of the nurse watching him and listening, said, "I love you, Mary."

He really did. More important, he sometimes thought, he liked her, too. Admired her. Enjoyed her company, her voice, her laugh, the way she touched him, the way she understood him. He was right, this decision he was making. And he'd made it without even being conscious of it. He would be wrong to lose her. Having made his decision, he set about confirming it—thinking of all the things that were wrong with his job, with the reservation, with the Navajo culture. Making comparisons: This hospital room and the cold discomfort of his grandmother's hogan; the security of life with a regular paycheck and the sheep rancher's endless nerve-wracking dependence on rain that wouldn't fall, comparing the comforts of white society with the unemployment and poverty of the People. Perversely, these thoughts led him to the Silver Threads, and Mr. Berger, and the woman whose son was coming to see her, and to the old women who lived on Jacaranda Street, Bentwoman Tsossie and Bentwoman's Daughter.

In fact, it was three days before he could get out of the hospital. The next day the headache returned, fierce and persistent. That provoked

another round of X-rays and a renewed verdict
that he was suffering from concussion. Mary
called in the afternoon and had to be persuaded
again not to drop everything and visit him. The
following day he felt fine, but the doctors
weren't finished with some test or other. Shaw
dropped in and reported he had nothing to report. Vaggan had proved surprisingly invisible.
He was suspected of being involved in a bizarre
assault case involving one of Southern California's television personalities; the description fit
and it seemed to involve a welshed bet, which
was the sort of work Vaggan did. But there was
no hard proof. A witness hadn't gotten a look at
him, and the victim and his girlfriend reported
he was wearing a stocking mask. He dropped a
copy of the Los Angeles *Times* on Chee's bed so
he could read about it. Shaw looked tired and
defeated.

Driving home the next day, Chee felt the same
way. He also felt depressed, nervous, frustrated,
irritated, and generally miles from that condition for which the Navajo word is *hozro*. It
means a sort of blend of being in harmony with
one's environment, at peace with one's circumstances, content with the day, devoid of anger,
and free from anxieties. Chee thought of his
neglected studies to become a *yataalii*, a shaman whose work it would be to restore his fel-

low Navajos to *hozro*. Physician, heal thyself, he thought. He drove eastward on Interstate 40 faster than he should, glum and disgruntled. Mary Landon hung in his mind—a problem he had solved but which refused to stay solved. And when he turned away from that, it was to the frustration of the postcard, which seemed to have come from no one to Albert Gorman, and on to Ashie Begay, and then to disappear—unless Margaret Sosi had it.

Chee stopped at a Flagstaff motel. The weathercast at the close of the ten o'clock news was on, the map showing a high-pressure area centered over northern Utah that promised to hold winter at bay for at least another day. Chee fell into bed, tired but not sleepy, and found himself reviewing it again.

Simple enough on the Los Angeles end. A car-theft operation broken, some indicted, some persuaded to be witnesses. One was Leroy Gorman. That much seemed sure. Leroy Gorman tucked away under the Witness Protection Program under the name of Grayson, and denying he was Gorman because the Federals had told him to deny it. If Shaw's information was correct, Albert Gorman had refused to cooperate. Upchurch had nothing to scare him with. But something—apparently that photograph/postcard of the trailer—had caused Albert to decide to come to Shiprock to find his brother. He'd been pursued. Why? Presumably because his employers wanted him to lead them to Leroy so that Leroy could be eliminated as a witness. Albert Gorman had resisted. Albert Gorman had been shot.

Chee lay listening to the truck traffic rumble on the Interstate, thinking of that. One odd hole in the Los Angeles end. Albert Gorman hadn't been followed to Shiprock. They'd known he was going there. Lerner had flown directly to Farmington and driven directly to Shiprock. And if what Berger had told him was true, Vaggan had come to Gorman's apartment to keep him from going to Shiprock. So much for that. So much for the reasonable, logical explanation. But at least he knew now why Lerner had gone to do the dirty work instead of Vaggan. Vaggan was having a splint put on a finger broken when Albert slammed the car door on it. Fat lot that helped.

Chee groaned, punched the pillow into better shape, rolled over. Nothing fit. Tomorrow morning he'd call Captain Largo, and tell him he'd be back in Shiprock by midafternoon, and see if Largo had learned anything while Chee was wasting his time in California. And he would complain about his headache and ask for a week of sick leave. He had some work he wanted to do.

≫ **22** ≪

FROM FLAGSTAFF, NEAR THE WESTERN EDGE of the Navajo Big Reservation, to Shiprock, near its northern border, is about 230 miles if you take the most direct route through Tuba City. Chee took that route, checking out of his motel before sunrise and stopping briefly at Gray Mountain to call Largo.

First he dealt with official business. He was going to apply for a week of sick leave to let his head heal. Would it be approved? All right, Largo said, sounding neutral.

He'd told Largo in a call from the hospital the basics about what had happened to him and what he'd learned. Now he told him a little more, including what Shaw had learned, or failed to learn, in his visit to the U.S.D.A.'s office. "Shaw doesn't have any doubt that this Grayson is really Leroy Gorman," Chee said. "Neither do I. But it would be a good thing to confirm it. Is there a way you could do that? Find out for sure he's a protected witness?"

"He is," Largo said.

"You checked?"

"I checked," Largo said. "Grayson is Leroy Gorman. Or I should say Leroy Gorman is Grayson and will be until they haul him back to Los Angeles and have him testify. Then he'll be Leroy Gorman again."

Chee wanted to ask Largo how he'd found out. Obviously the FBI would not tell Largo or anyone else anything about this supersecret witness business. It was a long-time sore point with the local law that the Federals moved all sorts of known felons into their jurisdiction under false identities with no warning to anybody. The Justice Department said it was essential to the safety of witnesses. Local law saw the insult built into it—another statement from the Federals that locals couldn't be trusted. So how had Largo checked? The first possibility that occurred to Chee was a visit to the local telephone office to find out who ordered the telephone line connected to the trailer.

"Is Sharkey paying Grayson's telephone bill?" Chee asked.

Largo chuckled. "He is. And the bill for hauling that trailer in there from Farmington—the hauling company sent that right to the FBI. But when I told Sharkey what we know about all this, you'd have thought he couldn't imagine why I thought he'd be interested."

"Well," Chee said. "I'll see you next week."

"When you come back to work," Largo said, "I want you to make one more try to find that Sosi girl. And this time handcuff her to your steering wheel or something to get her to hold still long enough to find out about that postcard. You think you can do that?"

Chee said he could try, and he asked the captain to switch him to the dispatcher.

"Dispatcher?" Largo said.

"Yeah," Chee said. "If I haven't had any mail, I'll skip coming in."

Largo switched the call.

Chee didn't have any mail. He hadn't expected to. Then he arranged to have a horse saddled and a horse trailer ready for him for the afternoon. Captain Largo could have arranged that, but Captain Largo would have wanted to know why he wanted the horse.

Outside the Gray Mountain store, Chee stretched, yawned, and sucked in a huge lungful of air. It was cold here, frost still riming the roadside weeds, and the snowcapped shape of the San Francisco Peaks twenty miles to the south looked close enough to touch in the clear, high-altitude air. The winter storm being held at

bay by the Utah high in last night's weathercast
was still hung up somewhere over the horizon.
The only clouds this morning were high-
altitude cirrus so thin that the blue showed
through them. Beautiful to Chee. He was back
in Dine' Bike'yah, back Between the Sacred
Mountains, and he felt easy again—at home in
a remembered landscape. He stood beside his
pickup, postponing for a moment the four or
five hours he still had to spend driving, and
studied the mountain. It was something Frank
Sam Nakai had instructed him to do. "Memorize places," his uncle had told him. "Settle your
eyes on a place and learn it. See it under the
snow, and when first grass is growing, and as
the rain falls on it. Feel it and smell it, walk on
it, touch the stones, and it will be with you forever. When you are far away, you can call it
back. When you need it, it is there, in your
mind."

This was one of those places for Chee—this
desert sloping away to the hills that rose to
become Dook'o'oosli'id, Evening Twilight
Mountain, the Mountain of the West, the mountain built by First Man as the place where the
holy Abalone Shell Boy would live, guarded by
the Black Wind *yei*. He had memorized this
place when he worked out of the Tuba City
agency. He leaned his elbows against the roof of

his pickup and memorized it again, with rags of fog drifting away from the snowy peaks and the morning sun making slanting shadows across the foothills. "Touch it with your mind," Frank Sam Nakai had told him. "Inhale the air that moves across it. Listen to the sounds it makes." The sounds this place was making this morning were the sounds of crows, hundreds of them, moving out of the trees around the trading post back toward wherever this flock spent its winter days.

Chee climbed back into the truck and rolled it onto U.S. 89 North. He wanted to get where he had to go a long time before dark.

He got there about midafternoon, driving steadily and fast despite a quickening north wind, which told him the storm was finally bulging down out of Utah. He made a quick stop at his trailer in Shiprock to strap on his pistol, get his heavy coat, and collect a loaf of bread and what was left of a package of bologna. He picked up the horse and trailer at the tribal barns and ate on the long bumpy drive back into the Chuskas, trailed now by a cold north wind. He parked where Albert Gorman had abandoned his ruined Plymouth, unloaded the horse, and rode the rest of the way to the Begay hogan. The sky was clouding now, a high gray overcast moving down from the northwest. Chee tied the horse in the shelter of Begay's empty corral and quickly scouted the hogan yard. If anyone had been here since he'd left the place, they'd left no sign. Then he walked around the hogan to its broken north wall.

The wind was gusty now, whipping dust around his feet and making sibilant noises in the corpse hole. Chee squatted and peered inside. In the gray light of the stormy afternoon, he could see just what he'd seen by the light of his flash when he'd been here before: the rusty iron stove, the stove pipe connecting it to the smoke hole, odds and ends of trash. The wind hooted through the hole and sent a scrap of paper scuttling across the hard-packed earthen floor. The wind eddied around the collar of his padded coat, touching his neck with cold. Chee shivered and pulled the collar tight. By Navajo tradition, Albert Gorman now would have completed his journey to the underworld, would have vanished into the dark unknown which the metaphysics of the People had never tried to explain or explore. But his *chindi* would be here, an unhappy, discordant, malevolent evil—whatever in Gorman had been out of harmony—trapped forever inside the hogan when Gorman had died.

Chee took a deep breath and stepped through the hole.

He was instantly aware that it was warmer inside, and of the smell of dust and of something sharper. He paused a moment, trying to identify the aroma. Old grease, old ashes, old sweat—the smell of human occupation. Chee opened the stove door. Nothing in the oven. He opened the fire box. The ashes had already been stirred, probably by Sharkey. He picked up the scrap of paper the wind had moved. A torn bit of old envelope with nothing written on it. He found the place at the west side of the hogan where Begay had habitually laid his sheepskins for sleeping. He took out his knife and dug into the packed earth, looking for he knew not what. He found nothing at all, and paused, squatting on his heels, thinking.

Jim Chee was aware of the sound of the wind outside, whispering around the corpse hole and at the blocked smoke hole over his head. He was very much aware of the ghost of Albert Gorman in the air around him, and suddenly he was aware, clearly and surely, of the nature of the Gorman *chindi*. Like Gorman—of course like Gorman since it was Gorman—it was Los Angeles, and the little girl whores he'd seen along Sunset Boulevard, and the impersonal precision of the herds on the freeways, and the chemical gray air, and Albert Gorman's landlady, and the pink-faced aide at the Silver Threads. And now it was Jim Chee's ghost because Jim Chee had chosen it—stepped through the corpse hole into the darkness freely and willingly, having decided to do so rationally. Having chosen Los Angeles over Shiprock, and Mary Landon over the loneliness and poverty and beauty of *hozro*. Chee squatted on his heels, and looked around him, and tried to think of what he should be looking for. Instead, he remembered the song from the hogan blessing ceremonial.

This hogan will be a blessed hogan.
It will become a hogan of dawn,
Dawn Boy will live in beauty in it,
It will be a hogan of white corn,
It will be a hogan of soft goods,
It will be a hogan of crystal water,
It will be a hogan dusted with pollen,
It will be a hogan of long-life happiness,
It will be a hogan with beauty above it,
It will be a hogan with beauty all around it.

The words of Talking God came back to Chee. They would have been sung here, when Begay's family had gathered to help him bless this hogan a long time ago. Chee got to his feet, took out his knife again, and walked to the east wall. Here, under the end of the base log just atop the foundation stones, the singer hired by Ashie Begay to conduct his hogan ceremonial would have placed a choice piece of Begay's turquoise.

Chee chipped away with the knife tip at the dried adobe plaster, dislodged a chunk of it, and crumbled it in his fingers. The turquoise was there, a polished oval of clear blue gemstone. Chee wiped it on his shirt, inspected it, and put it back under the log. He walked to the west wall, dug under the end of the foundation log, and extracted a white seashell. The abalone shell symbolized the great *yei* Abalone Boy, just as the turquoise represented the Turquoise Boy spirit. But what had finding them told him? Nothing, Chee thought, that he hadn't believed he knew—that Begay was orthodox, that this hogan had been properly blessed, that Begay, in abandoning his home, had left these ritual jewels behind. Would that be orthodox? Probably, Chee thought. Unless Begay had thought to remove them before Albert Gorman died they wouldn't be removed at all—just as no wood from this hogan would ever be used again, not even for a fire. But removing them before Gorman died would have been prudent, and Begay must have seen the death coming, and Bentwoman had described her grandson as a prudent man. What would a prudent man salvage from his hogan if he saw death approaching it?

What had Bentwoman expected him to find in here?

Of course! Chee walked around the stove to the east-facing entrance. He felt along the log lintel above the door, running his fingers through the accumulated dust. Nothing. He tried to the right of the door. There, his fingers probing into the space over the log encountered something.

Chee held it in his left hand, a small brown pouch of dusty doeskin tied at the top with a leather thong. His fingers squeezed it, feeling exactly what he expected to feel. The pouch contained four soft objects. Chee untied the thong and dumped into his palm four smaller pouches, also of doeskin. He held Ashie Begay's Four Mountains Bundle.

The instant he saw it, he knew that Ashie Begay was dead.

Chee stepped through the corpse hole into snow. The wind now was carrying small, light flakes, which blew across the yard of Ashie Begay's hogan as dry as dust. He climbed down to the corral, the Four Mountains Bundle tucked in his coat pocket, to where he had tied his horse—thinking about what he'd found. The bundle represented weeks of work, a pilgrimage to each of the four sacred mountains to collect from each the herbs and minerals pre-

scribed by the Holy People. Chee had collected
his own the summer of his junior year at the
University of New Mexico. Mount Taylor and
the San Francisco Peaks had been easy enough,
thanks to access roads to Forest Service fire
lookouts on both of their summits. But Blanca
Peak in the Sangre de Cristos and Hesperus
Peak in the Las Platas had been a different matter. Begay would have gone through that ordeal
in harder times, before roads led into the high
country. Or he might have inherited it from his
family. Either way, he would never have left it
behind in a death hogan. It would have been his
most treasured belonging, an heirloom beyond
price.

So what had happened at Ashie Begay's
hogan?

Chee had brought the horse because he intended, no matter what he might find in the
hogan, to make a general search of Ashie
Begay's home territory. Now that search took
on new purpose. The horse stomped and whin-
nied as he approached, cold and ready to move.
Chee untied it, dusted the snow off its haunches,
and swung into the saddle. What had happened
at this hogan? Could Begay have gone away,
returned to find Gorman dead, and forgot the
sacred pouch when he abandoned the hogan?

That was inconceivable. So what had happened?

Had someone else come after Albert Gorman after Lerner had failed to stop him, and found him at Ashie Begay's hogan, and killed them both, and then taken the time for Gorman's ceremonial burial, emptying the hogan and hiding Begay's body? Chee considered that. Possibly. In fact, something like that must have happened. But what would be the motive? He could think of none that made sense.

Chee circled the hogan yard and then rode east on a sheep trail leading down the arroyo rim. He rode slowly, looking for anything that might deviate in any way from normal. After more than a mile of finding absolutely nothing, he trotted the horse back to the hogan yard. It was snowing more heavily now and the temperature was dropping sharply. The second trail he tried led up past the talus slope, past the place where Gorman's body had been left, and followed under the cliff west of the hogan. It took him into the wind, making the horse reluctant and visibility difficult. He pulled his hatbrim down and rode with head bowed to keep the snowflakes out of his eyes—plodding along studying the ground, knowing what he was looking for without letting the thought take any exact shape in his mind. The snow was sticking,

accumulating fast. Soon it would cover everything and make his search futile. He should
have done this long ago. Should have used his
head. Should have attended his instinctive
knowledge that Hosteen Ashie Begay would not
have abandoned this place to a ghost, would not
have left his nephew half prepared for the journey to the underworld. There was this trail to
check out, and at least two more, and there
wouldn't be time to do it all before the snow
covered everything.

There almost wasn't time.

Chee saw the horse without realizing he was
seeing anything more than a round boulder
coated with snow. But there was something a
little wrong with the color where the snow
hadn't stuck, a redness that was off-key for the
gray granite of this landscape. He pulled up on
the reins, and wiped the snowflakes out of his
eyebrows, and stared. Then he climbed down
out of the saddle. He saw the second horse only
when he'd walked down into the trail-side gully
to inspect the first one.

Whoever had shot them had led them both far
enough down from the trail so that, if they had
both fallen as he must have intended, they
would have been out of sight. But the one Chee
had seen apparently hadn't cooperated. It was a
big bay gelding, and the bullet fired into its fore-

head apparently had touched off a frantic struggle. It had lunged uphill, two or three bounding reflex jumps judging from the dislodged stones, before its brain turned off in death.

Hosteen Begay's belongings were dumped out of sight farther down the wash, behind a screen of piñons. Chee sorted through them quickly, identifying bedding, clothing, boxes of cooking utensils, and two sacks of food. Begay's furniture was also here. A kitchen chair, a cot, a light chest of drawers, enough other odds and ends of living to convince Chee that even with two horses hauling, it must have taken more than one trip to move it all here. He stood beside the cache and looked around. This was what he'd expected, had expected since his mind had time to calculate what finding the Four Mountains Bundle had meant. He'd expected it, but it still left him sick. And there was one more thing to be found.

He found Ashie Begay a bit farther down the wash, his body dumped as unceremoniously as the furniture. Begay had been shot in the head, just like his horses.

> 23 <

It took chee three hours to get his pickup out of the Chuskas. Twice it involved digging through drifts, and twice he had to unload the horse and lead it up slopes where the truck lacked the traction to pull the load. By the time he reached the graded road leading to the Toadlena boarding school he was weary to the bone, with another thirteen miles through the snow to Highway 666 and thirty more to Shiprock. The snow blew steadily from the north-north-west, and he drove northward alternately through a narrow white tunnel formed by his headlights reflecting off the driven flakes and brief blinding oblivions of ground blizzards. His radio told him that Navajo Route 1 was closed from Shiprock south to Kayenta, and Navajo Route 3 was closed from Two Story to Keams Canyon, and that U.S. 666 was closed from Mancos Creek, Colorado, to Gallup, New Mexico. That helped

explain why Chee's pickup truck had the highway to itself. He drove about twenty-five miles
an hour, slowing as well as he could when he
sensed the ground blizzards coming, his fingers
sensitive to traction under his wheels and his
shoulder muscles aching with fatigue. He'd covered the body of Hosteen Ashie Begay with
Begay's bedroll, thinking that he, like Gorman,
had had to make his journey into the underworld with his hair unwashed—without even
the imperfect preparations Gorman's corpse
had received. But the man who killed him had
at least sent along with Begay the spirits of his
horses. Had he known that sacrifice of the
owner's horse had been an ancient Navajo custom? Possibly. But Chee had no illusions that
this was why the horses had been killed. They
were killed for the same reason Begay was
killed, and his hogan emptied, and Gorman's
corpse prepared for burial—a great deal of trouble to make it seem that nothing unusual had
happened at Begay's hogan. But why? Why?
Why?

There seemed to Chee to be little enough mystery about who the killer was. It was Vaggan, or
some surrogate Vaggan—one of those who, in
white society, did such things for pay. But it was
probably the man Shaw had identified as Vaggan. This seemed to be his job, whatever its pur-

pose. And it would have been easy enough to learn about Navajo burial customs. They would be covered in any of a half-dozen books available in the Los Angeles library. Anyone who could read could have learned enough to fake what had happened at the Begay hogan. Who had done it didn't matter—Vaggan or someone like him. The question was why.

Chee was finding he couldn't make his mind work very well. The headache had returned. Fatigue, probably, and eyestrain induced from staring into the reflecting snow. He put Begay's body out of his consciousness and thought only about driving. And finally there to his right was the sign indicating the entrance road to the Shiprock landing strip, and he could feel the highway sloping downward into the San Juan river bottom, and Shiprock was just ahead.

He turned the horse into the shelter of the tribal barn, and left the horse trailer in the lot, and drove into the village. Across the bridge he hesitated a moment. A left turn at the junction would take him to his trailer home, to hot coffee, food, his bed. To a telephone to report to Captain Largo what he had found. To deal again with the question of why. The postcard would come up again. Inevitably. It lay at the center of all of this. Had, apparently, triggered it. What had been written on that postcard? Chee turned right, downriver toward the place where the aluminum trailer was parked under a cottonwood tree.

It looked different, somehow, in this storm. Before temperatures had dropped, snow had crusted on the cold aluminum and collected more snow, and cost the trailer its machine-made look. It loomed in Chee's headlights now as a great white shape, tied to the earth by a drift, as natural as a snow-caked boulder and looking as if it had stood below its tree forever. Light glowed from the small windows. Grayson, or somebody, was home. Chee honked the pickup's horn and waited a moment before it occurred to him that Grayson was a city man who wouldn't be aware of this rural custom of giving warning before invading privacy. He turned up his coat collar and stepped out into the blowing snow.

If Grayson had heard his horn, there was no evidence of it. Chee rapped his knuckles against the aluminum door panel, waited, and rapped again. The wind worked under the bottom of his coat and around the collar and up his pants legs, as cold as death. It reminded Chee of the corpse of Hosteen Ashie Begay lying frozen under the old man's bedroll. And then the voice of Grayson, through the door.

"Who is it?"

"It's Chee," Chee shouted. "Navajo Police."

"What do you want?"

"We found your uncle's body," Chee said. "Ashie Begay. I need to talk to you."

Silence. The cold gripped Chee's ankles, numbed his cheeks. Then Grayson's voice shouted, "Come on in."

The door opened. It opened outward, as trailer doors open to conserve inside space, no more than six inches, and then the wind pushed it shut again. Chee stood a moment, looking at it, wondering what Grayson was doing and finally understanding. Grayson was playing it safe, as a protected witness might be expected to do. He opened the door and stepped in.

Grayson was sitting behind the table, his back against the wall, examining Chee. Chee shut the door and stood against it, enjoying the warmth and letting Grayson see his hands were empty.

"You found whose body?" Grayson said. "Where? What happened?"

Grayson's hands were out of sight beneath the table. Would he have a weapon? Would a protected witness be allowed to have a gun? Perhaps even be encouraged to keep one? Why not?

"Not far from his hogan," Chee said. "Somebody had shot him."

Grayson's face registered a kind of dismay. He looked a little older than Chee had remembered, a little more tired. Maybe it was the artificial light. More likely it was Chee's mood. The corner of his mouth pulled back in the beginning of one of those wry clicks of sympathy or surprise or sorrow, but Grayson stopped it. He brought his hands out from under the table, rubbed his face with the right one. The left one lay on the table, limp and empty. "Why would anyone want to kill that old man?" Grayson said.

"Your uncle," Chee said.

Grayson stared at him.

"We know who you are," Chee said. "It saves time if we get that out of the way. You're Leroy Gorman. You're in the Department of Justice Witness Protection Program under the name of Grayson. You're living here under the Grayson name until it's time to go back to Los Angeles to testify in federal court."

The man who was Leroy Gorman, older brother of Albert Gorman, nephew of Ashie Begay, stared at Chee, his expression blank. And bleak. And Chee thought, What is his real name? His war name? The name his maternal uncle would have given him, privately and secretly when he was a child, the name he would have whispered through the mask at the Yeibichi ceremonial where he changed from boy to man? The name that would label his real identity, that no one would know except those closest to him, what was that? This Los Angeles Navajo doesn't have a war name, Chee thought, because he doesn't have a family. He isn't Dinee. He felt pity for Leroy Gorman. Part of it was fatigue, and part of it was pity for himself.

"So much for the goddam promises," Leroy Gorman said. "Nobody knows but one guy in the Prosecutor's office and your FBI guardian angel. That's what they tell you. Nobody else. Not the local fuzz. Not nobody, so there's no way it can leak." He rapped his hand sharply on the Formica tabletop. "Who'd they tell? They have something about it on TV? Front page of the *Times?* On the radio?"

"They didn't tell anybody as far as I know," Chee said. "The postcard you wrote gave you away. The one you sent to your brother."

"I didn't write any postcard," Gorman said.

"Let me see your camera," Chee said.

"Camera?" Gorman looked surprised. He stood, opened the overhead cabinet behind him, and extracted a camera from its contents. It was a Polaroid model with a flash attachment. Chee inspected it. It was equipped with an automatic timer.

"Not exactly a postcard," Chee said. "You set this thing up, and took a picture of yourself and this trailer house, and sent it to your brother.

Whatever you wrote on it, it caused him to come running out here to Shiprock looking for you. And when Old Man Begay saw it, something on it, or something Albert told him, caused him to send it along to his granddaughter to tell her to stay away."

Gorman was looking at him, thinking. He shook his head.

"What did you write on it?" Chee asked.

"Nothing, really," Gorman said. "I don't remember, exactly. I just figured Al would be worried about me. Just wrote a little note. Like wish you were here."

"Did you say where 'here' was?"

"Hell, no," Gorman said.

"Just a little note," Chee said. "Then what do you think it was that brought your brother running?"

Gorman thought. He clicked his tongue. "Maybe," he said, "maybe he heard something I need to know about."

"Like what?" Chee said.

"I dunno," Gorman said. "Maybe he heard they were looking for me. Maybe he heard they knew where to find me."

That had a plausible sound. Albert had heard Leroy's hiding place had leaked. When Leroy's card arrived, he'd seen the Shiprock postmark and had hurried here to warn his brother and hadn't quite made it. And then someone had been sent to make sure that Albert Gorman didn't survive his gunshot wound. How had Albert Gorman really died? The coroner had said gunshot wound, which was obvious and what they'd expected, and what they'd have looked for. But if they were looking for something else, what would they have found? That Albert Gorman had been suffocated, or something like that, which didn't show but would hurry the death from the gunshot wound along? Or had whoever had come to the hogan found him already dead and killed Ashie Begay because of what Albert might have told him? It didn't really matter. Chee's head ached, his eyes burned. He was thinking maybe Albert Gorman died outside the hogan after all. Maybe he hadn't stepped through the corpse hole into a *chindi* hogan. Maybe he wasn't contaminated with ghost sickness. But that didn't matter either. The ghost sickness came when he made the step—out of *hozro* and into the darkness. Out of being a Navajo, into being a white man. For Chee, that was where the sickness lay.

"Any idea who killed him," Leroy Gorman asked, "or why?"

"No," Chee said. "Do you?"

Gorman was slumped back in his chair, his hands on the table in front of him, looking over them at nothing. He sighed, and the wind out-side picked up enough to remind them both of the storm. "Could be just meanness," Gorman said. He sighed again. "Did you find that girl?"

"Not exactly," Chee said.

"I don't guess she'll be coming here," Gorman said. "Didn't you say her grandfather told her to stay away? Something dangerous?"

"Yeah," Chee said. "But it didn't stop her the first time."

"What did he tell her?" Gorman was still look-ing past his hands, his eyes on the door. The wind pressed against it, letting in the cold. "She know I'm a car thief?"

"I don't know what he told her," Chee said. "I intend to find out."

"She's kinfolk of mine," Gorman said. "I don't have many. Not much family. Just Al and me. Dad run off and our mother was sickly and we never got to know nobody. She's my niece, isn't she? Begay's granddaughter. That'd be my mother's sister. I knew she had one out here somewhere. I remember she mentioned that. Wonder if that aunt of mine would still be alive. Wonder where that little girl went."

Chee didn't comment. He wanted a cup of coffee badly. And food, and sleep. He tried to think of what else he could ask this man, what he could possibly learn that would keep this from being just another in a long line of dead ends. He could think of nothing.

"I'd like to get acquainted with her," Leroy Gorman said. "Meet her family. I didn't make much of a white man. Maybe when I get through with all this I could make some sort of Navajo. You know where I could find the Sosi family?"

Chee shook his head. He got up and thanked Leroy Gorman for his time and went through the aluminum door into the driving snow, leaving Gorman sitting there looking at his hands, his face full of thought.

> 24 <

HE CALLED LARGO from his trailer while the coffee perked and told the captain what he had found at Begay's hogan. It took Largo something like a micromillisecond to get over his sleepiness and then he was full of questions, not all of which Chee could answer. Finally that part of it was over, and it was a little after 2 A.M. and Chee was full of hot coffee, and two sandwiches, and in bed, and asleep almost before he could appreciate the sound of the winter outside.

He awoke with the sun on his face. The storm had moved fast, as early winter storms tend to move in the Mountain West, and had left in its wake a cold, bright stillness. Chee took his time. He warmed himself some leftover mutton stew for his breakfast and ate it with corn tortillas and refried beans. He ate slowly and a lot, because he had a lot to do and a long way to go, and whether or not he had another hot meal this day would depend on road conditions. He put on his thermal underwear, his wool socks, the boots he used for mud. He made sure that his tire chains were in the box behind the seat in his pickup, that his shovel, his hand winch, and his tow chain were in their proper places. He stopped at the gas station beside the San Juan bridge and topped off his gas tank and made sure the auxiliary tank was also full. And then he drove westward out of Shiprock to find Frank Sam Nakai. Nakai was his teacher, his friend since earliest boyhood, and, most important of all in the Navajo scheme of things, the brother of his mother—his key clan uncle.

The first seventy miles, through Teec Nos Pos, Red Mesa, Mexican Water, and Dennehotso, was easy enough going over the snow-packed asphalt of Route 504. Beyond Dennehotso, reaching the winter hogan of Frank Sam Nakai involved turning southward off the highway on a dirt road that wandered across Greasewood Flats, dipped across the usually dry Tyende Creek Canyon, and then climbed Carson Mesa. Five miles down this doubtful route, Chee decided it wasn't going to work. The air was still cold but the hot sun was turning the snow pack into mush. He had put his chains on before he left the highway, but even with them, the truck slipped and slid. As the day wore on it would get steadily worse until sundown froze it all again. He made it back to the highway and made the hundred-mile circle back through Mexican Water and southward to Round Rock and Many Farms and Chinle, and then the long, slippery way to the south side of Black Mesa past the Cottonwood Day School and through Blue Gap, to an old road which led to Tah Chee Wash. It was as bad as the road south from Dennehotso but, from where the passable stretch ended near Blue Gap, much shorter. Chee drove down it in second, at a cautious ten miles an hour. He'd drive as far as the melting snow would allow, walk in the remaining miles, and walk out again when the cold darkness turned the snow into ice and the mud into frozen iron.

The walking part turned out to be a little less than ten miles—a hard four hours in the soft snow. It gave Chee time to think, to sort it all out again. It resolved itself into a single central puzzle. Why had someone gone to so much trouble to conceal the murder of Ashie Begay? Chee could understand why Gorman might have been followed to the Begay hogan. That simply continued the effort to find Leroy Gorman. McNair, somehow, seemed to have learned that Leroy was in Shiprock, learned that Albert was going there, decided that Albert's arrival would scare the FBI into moving Leroy before his exact location could be pinned down, and sent someone to catch Albert and learn from Albert where Leroy could be found. Albert had resisted, been wounded, fled. Albert had been tracked down at Begay's place by someone (probably Vaggan) seeking an answer to the same question. Vaggan had either found Albert dead, or dying, or had killed him, and had killed Ashie Begay to eliminate a witness to the crime.

That was all plausible enough. It left questions, true. How had Vaggan found Albert Gorman so quickly at the Begay hogan? Probably because the McNair people knew enough about Albert's connections on the reservation to make an educated guess. After all, one of those involved was a Navajo: Beno. Robert Beno, Upchurch had said. High enough in the organization to warrant grand jury action, and the only one who managed to run. Another relative, perhaps. Another member of the Turkey Clan. Someone who could guess the only place Albert Gorman could find refuge. Or maybe it was simpler than that. Albert surely had intended to visit his uncle when he came to the reservation—to Chee's Navajo mind such a visit by a nephew was certain and inevitable—and he had told Mrs. Day, who had passed the information along. Anyway, that didn't seem to matter. What mattered was why all the trouble to make the crime at Begay's hogan invisible.

Chee plodded along through ankle-deep snow, examining possibilities. Because Vaggan didn't want the law to know he was looking for Leroy and was within a hundred miles of finding him? That looked good for a moment, but the shooting in the parking lot had already alerted the FBI. What other motive could there be? Chee could think of none and skipped over to another question. If the McNair people knew, or even suspected, that Leroy was hidden away in Shiprock, why weren't they looking for him? Largo had said there was no sign at all of that. No strangers asking around. Largo had put the word out, at the gas stations, and trading posts, and convenience stores, the post office, the laundry, everywhere. It was an old and simple and absolutely efficient system, and Chee had no doubt that if anyone—anyone at all—had shown up in Shiprock, or anywhere near Shiprock, asking questions, Largo would have known it within fifteen minutes. And unless McNair knew about the aluminum trailer and had some idea of where it was parked, Leroy Gorman couldn't be found without questions—hundreds of them. Chee had hunted enough people on the reservation to know how many weary hours of questions. And if McNair did know about the aluminum trailer and the cottonwood tree, Leroy would have been found with no questions at all. And Leroy would be just as dead as Albert.

And so the thinking went, leading around in the same circle back to the picture of the aluminum trailer mailed as a postcard with something, apparently, written on its back that had brought Albert running and started all this. Something, even though Leroy didn't remember writing such a stirring message—or claimed he didn't remember it. What would Leroy have written that he'd refuse to admit? Chee would know, he hoped, when he found Margaret Billy Sosi again—for the third time—and pinned her down long enough to extract from her either the card itself or her exact and detailed memory of what was written on it, and what her grandfather had told her about why Gorman (which Gorman?) was dangerous to be around. And just about when Chee was thinking this, he smelled smoke.

It was the smell of burning piñon, the sweet, perfumed smell of hot resin. Then a blue wisp of the smoke against the junipers on the next hillside, and the place of Frank Sam Nakai was in view. It was an octagonal log hogan, a rectangular frame house covered with black tarpaper, a flatbed truck, a green pickup, a corral with a sheep pen built beyond it, the tin building where Nakai kept his cattle feed, and, off against the hillside, the square plank building where the mother of Frank Sam Nakai's late wife lived with Frank Sam Nakai's daughter. The smoke was coming from stovepipes in both houses, making wisps of blue as separate as the suppers the occupants were cooking. Chee's uncle and his uncle's mother-in-law were following the instructions of Changing Woman, who had taught that when men look upon the mothers of the women they marry it may cause blindness and other more serious problems. To Jim Chee it seemed perfectly natural.

It also seemed natural to Chee that Frank Sam Nakai was absolutely delighted to see him. Nakai had been shoveling snow into barrels, where the sun would convert it into drinking water, when he saw Chee approaching. His shout of welcome brought Chee's aunt out of the house. His aunt by white man's reckoning was Mrs. Frank Sam Nakai. Her Navajo friends, neighbors, and clansmen called her Blue Woman in honor of her spectacular turquoise jewelry. But to Chee she was and always had been and would be Little Mother, and in honor of his visit she opened cans of peaches and candied yams to augment the spicy mutton tacos she served him for his supper. Only when all that was finished, and the utensils cleared from the table, and news of all the family covered, did Chee bring up what had brought him here.

"My father," he said to Frank Sam Nakai, "how many *yataalii* are left who know how to cure someone of the ghost sickness?"

Behind him, where she was sitting beside the stove, Chee heard Little Mother draw in her breath. His uncle digested the question.

"There are two ways it can be done," he said finally. "There is the nine-day sing and the five-day. I think not many know the nine-day any more. Maybe only an old man who lives up by Navajo Mountain. Up in Utah. You could find somebody to do the five-day cure a little easier. There was a man who knew it, I remember, when we were teaching young people to be *yataalii* at the Navajo Community College. I remember he said he learned it from his uncle, and his uncle lived over on the Moenkopi Plateau, over there by Dinnebito Wash. So that would be two. But the uncle was old even then. Maybe he is dead by now."

"How could I find this man? The younger one?"

"Tomorrow we will go to Ganado. To the college. They kept a list there of everybody who knew the sings, and where they lived." His uncle's face was asking the question that his courtesy would never allow him to put in words. Who suffered from ghost sickness? Was the victim Jim Chee?

"I'm trying to find a girl of the Turkey Clan who people call Margaret Billy Sosi," Chee said. "She was in a *chindi* hogan, and I think she will be having a sing." He heard a sigh from Little Mother, a sound of relief. He didn't want to tell these two that he, too, was infected. He didn't want to tell his uncle what he had done. He didn't want to tell him that he was going to get a job with the FBI, and leave the People, and give up his idea of being a *yataalii* like his uncle. He didn't want to see the sadness in that good man's face.

They'd had coffee and bread and had three horses saddled before it was time for his uncle to take a pinch of pollen and a pinch of meal and go out to bless the rising sun with the prayer to Dawn Boy. Little Mother rode with them to lead their horses back, and everything went very rapidly. The drive back over the now-frigid snow was like driving over ground glass, squeaking and crunching under Chee's tires. They were on the good road past Blue Gap in thirty minutes. Before noon, they were in the library at Navajo Community College, working their way through the roster of men and women who are shamans of the Navajos.

Chee hadn't known it existed. He should have known, he thought. It would be useful to any policeman. And even while he was thinking that, another part of his consciousness was shocked and dismayed. So few names. And so many of them listed as knowing only the Blessing Way, or the Enemy Way, or the Yeibichi, the Night Chant, or the more common and popular curing rituals. He glanced at Frank Sam Nakai, who was running his finger slowly down the page. His uncle had told him that the Holy People had taught the Dinee at least sixty such rituals, and that many of them were lost in those grim years when the People had been herded into captivity at Fort Sumner. And he could see by this that more were being lost. He looked down the list to see how many singers knew the Stalking Way, which he had been trying to learn. He saw only the name of his uncle and one other man.

"Just two know the Ghostway," his uncle said. "That fellow I told you about and his old uncle, way over there west of Hopi country. Just two."

"It would probably be the younger man," Chee said. "The Turkey Clan seems to be eastern Navajos—mostly on this side of the Chuskas."

"You can see why we need you," Frank Sam

Nakai said. "Everybody is forgetting every-thing. There won't be anybody left to cure any-body. Nobody to keep us being Navajos."

"Yeah," Chee said. "That's the way it looks." He'd have to tell Frank Sam Nakai soon. Very soon. But today he just couldn't do it.

The fellow who knew the Ghostway (and the Blessing Way and Mountaintop Way) was on the book as Leo Littleben, Junior. And he lived not way the hell a thousand miles down a dirt track on the other side of the reservation but at Two Story, just twenty-five miles down the high-way toward Window Rock. And—rarity of rari-ties on the reservation—he was listed in the Navajo-Hopi telephone book.

"I think my luck's changing," Chee said.

Somebody answered the telephone at the Lit-tleben residence. A woman.

"He's not here," she said.

"When do you expect him back?" Chee asked.

"I don't know. Three-four more days, I think."

"Anyplace I can reach him?"

"He's doing a sing."

"Do you know where?"

"Way over there on the Cañoncito Reserva-tion."

His luck hadn't changed much, Chee thought. Cañoncito was as far as you could get from Ganado and still be in Navajo country. It was a fragment of reservation separated from the Big Reservation by miles of private land and by the Acoma and Laguna Indian reservations. It was practically in Albuquerque. In fact, it was outside Dine' Bike'yah, on the wrong side of the Turquoise Mountain. Some strictly orthodox medicine men would refuse to hold a sing there.

"Do you know who it's for?" Chee said. "Who hired him?"

"For some woman named Sosi, I think it is."

"A Ghostway?"

"A Ghostway," the woman agreed. "He's doing the five-day sing. Be back in another three-four days."

So Chee's luck had changed, after all.

> 25 <

It was almost dark when Chee turned off Exit
131 from Interstate 40 and took the worn asphalt that led northward. For the first miles the
road ran between fences bearing the No Tres-
passing signs of the Laguna Indian Pueblo—
grass country grazed by Herefords. But the land
rose, became rockier. More cactus now, and
more juniper and chamiza and saltbush, and
then a fading sign:

WELCOME TO THE CAÑONCITO RESERVATION
Home of the Cañoncito Band of Navajos
Population 1600

Leroy Gorman would have no trouble getting
this far, Chee thought, not if he could read road
signs well enough to navigate the Los Angeles
freeways. Chee had called him from the college,
using his Tribal Police identification number to
wring Grayson's unlisted number from the information operator's supervisor.

"You said you wanted to meet some kinfolks," Chee said. "You want to enough to drive a couple of hundred miles?"

"What else have I got to do?" Gorman said. "Where do I go?"

"South to Gallup. Then take Interstate forty east through Grants, and after you pass Laguna start looking for the Cañoncito Reservation interchange. Get off there and head into the reservation and look for the police station. I'll leave a map or something for you there to tell you where to go."

"You found the girl? They're having a curing thing for her?"

"Exactly," Chee said. "And the more of her relatives are there, the better it works."

Five miles beyond the entrance sign, a green steel prefabricated building, a shed, a mobile home, a parked semi-trailer, and a Phillips 66 gasoline sign marked the site of a trading post. Chee stopped. Anyone know the Sosi family? No Sosi family at Cañoncito. Anyone know where a sing was being held? Everybody did. It was way back on Mesa Gigante, at the place of Hosteen Jimmie Yellow. Easy to find it. How about the police station, where was that? Just down the road, three-four miles, before you get to the chapter house. Can't miss it.

It would, in fact, have been hard to miss—a

small frame building not fifty feet from the road wearing a sign that read simply POLICE STATION. It was manned, as Chee recalled the situation, not by the Navajo Tribal Police but by the Law and Order Division of the Bureau of Indian Affairs, a parttime patrolman who also worked the east side of Laguna territory. On this particular afternoon it was manned by a young woman wearing bifocals.

Chee showed her his identification. "I'm trying to find a sing they're having at Jimmie Yellow's place," Chee said. "You know how to get there?"

"Sure," the woman said. "Up on Mesa Gigante." She extracted a piece of typing paper from the desk, wrote *North* at the top of it and *East* on the right-hand side, and drew a tiny square near the bottom and labeled it *Cops*. Then she drew a line past the square northward. "This is Route Fifty-seven. Stay on it past"—she drew a cluster of tiny squares west of the line— "the chapter house and the Baptist Church off here, and then you angle westward on Road Seventy forty-five. There's a sign." The map took precise shape under her pen, with unwanted turns identified and blocked off with X's, and landmarks such as windmills, watertanks, and an abandoned coal mine properly indicated.

"Finally it winds around up here, under this

cliff, and then you're on top of the mesa. Only road up there so you don't have any choice. There's an old burned-out truck there right at the rim, and about a mile before you get to Yellow's place, you pass the ruins of an old hogan on the left. And you can see Yellow's place from the road."

"And I can't miss it," Chee said, grinning.

"I don't think so. It's the second turnoff, and the first one is to the old torn-down hogan." She looked up at him over her glasses, somberly. "Somebody died there, so nobody uses that track anymore. And after the turnoff to Yellow's place, that's all of them for miles because Jimmie Yellow's people are about the only ones up there any more."

Chee told her about Gorman driving down from Shiprock, instructed to stop here for directions. Would that be any problem? It wouldn't be. But as Chee drove away, he was nagged by a feeling that something would be a problem, that he was forgetting something, or overlooking something, or making some sort of mistake.

Jimmie Yellow's place, even more than Ashie Begay's, seemed to have been selected more for the view than for convenience. It was perched near the rim of the mesa, looking down into the great empty breaks that fell away to the Rio Puerco. To the west, across the Laguna Reservation, the snowy ridges of Turquoise Mountain reflected the light of the rising moon. To the east, the humped ridge of the Sandia Mountains rose against the horizon, their base lit by the glowing lights of Albuquerque. To the north, another line of white marked the snowcap on the Sangre de Cristo Mountains, and the bright smudge of yellow light below them was Santa Fe, one hundred miles away. A spectacular view, but no water, and only a scattered stand of juniper to provide firewood, and the snakeweed around Chee's boots indicated what too many sheep a long time ago had done to the grazing on the mesa top.

Still, the view was impressive, and normally Jim Chee would have enjoyed it and added it to his internal file of beautiful places memorized. Not tonight. Tonight, when Chee allowed himself to think of it, he looked at the mountains with a sense of loss. He had no illusions about where his career in the FBI would take him. They would identify him as an Indian, he was sure enough of that. And that would mean he'd be used in some apparently appropriate way. But they wouldn't send him home to work among people who were family, his kinsmen and clansmen. Too much risk of conflict of interest in that. He'd work in Washington, probably, at a desk coordinating the Agency's work with the Bureau of Indian Affairs. Or he'd be sent north to be a cop among the Cheyennes, or south to deal with federal crime on Seminole land in Florida. Aside from that dismal thought, Chee was not enjoying the view because he was not in the mood to enjoy anything. He had found Margaret Billy Sosi for the third time, and extracted from her the last missing piece of the puzzle, and it told him absolutely nothing.

He took Ashie Begay's Four Mountains Bundle from his coat pocket and tossed it in his hand. From behind him, the sound of a pot drum drifted on the cold, still air, and with it the sound of Littleben's voice, rising and falling in the chant which told how the Hero Twins had decided that Old Man Death must be spared and not eliminated in their campaign to cleanse Dinetah of its monsters. The same faint breeze which carried the sound brought the perfume of woodsmoke from the fire in the hogan, reminding Chee that it was warm in there, and that the cold out here at this slab of sandstone on which he was sitting was seeping into his bones. But he didn't want to be inside, sitting with his back to the hogan wall, watching Littleben build the last of the great sand paintings of this ceremonial, sharing the music and the poetry and the goodwill of these people. He wanted to be out here in the cold, trying to think, going over it all again.

He'd done his talking to Margaret Sosi when Littleben finished the segment that recounted how Monster Slayer and Born for Water had returned to the Earth Surface World with the weapons they had stolen from their father, the Sun. Littleben had come out of the hogan, wiping perspiration from his forehead, under the red headband, and looking curiously around him as people do who've been indoors too long. Then the others who were sharing in the blessing of the ceremony came out, and with them was Margaret Sosi, with her face covered with the blackening that made her invisible to ghosts. Margaret Sosi seemed exhausted and thin, but the eyes that looked out through the layer of soot were alive and excited. Margaret Sosi is being cured, Chee thought. Someday, perhaps, he could be.

Margaret Sosi was delighted to see him. She asked him about his head and told him he shouldn't be out of the hospital.

"I want to thank you for getting me there," Chee said. "How in the world did you do it?"

"When you hit him, he dropped his gun. I just picked it up and told him to take us to the hospital."

"As easy as that?"

Margaret Sosi shivered. "I was scared," she said. "I was scared to death."

"Before anything like that happens again," Chee said, "I need to ask you some questions. Did Hosteen Begay send you a postcard he'd gotten from Albert Gorman? A picture—"

"Yes," Margaret said.

"I'd like to see it."

"Sure," Margaret said. "But it's in my room. At St. Catherine. We went back there before we came here for the sing."

Of course, Chee thought. It wouldn't be here. He would never, ever actually see that postcard. Never.

"What did it say on it?"

Margaret Sosi frowned. "It just said, 'Don't trust nobody.' That's all. There was Mr. Gorman's name, and an address in Los Angeles, and that 'Don't trust nobody.' That's all there was. And at the bottom 'Leroy.' "

Chee didn't know what to say, so he said, "No return address?"

"No," Margaret said, "and not even a stamp. The postman had put that 'Postage Due' stamp on it."

"Well," Chee said. "Hell."

"Have you found my grandfather yet?"

Chee knew the question would be coming. He

had prepared himself for it. He had decided that the best thing for all concerned was simply to tell Margaret that her grandfather was dead. Straight out. Get it over with. He drew a deep breath. "Margaret," he said. "Uh, well . . ."

"He's dead, isn't he," Margaret Billy Sosi said. "I guess I knew it all along and just couldn't face it. I knew he would never abandon his hogan like that. Not and just go away with no word to anyone."

"Yes," Chee said. "He's dead."

Tears were streaking the soot on her face, a line of wetness that reflected the cold moonlight, but her voice didn't change. "Of course he was," she said. "Of course. He was killed, wasn't he? I guess I really knew it."

"And I don't think it was really a ghost hogan you were in," Chee added. "I think Gorman died outside. It was just made to look like Hosteen Begay had buried him, and broke the hogan wall, and abandoned it. So nobody would be looking around for him."

"But why?"

"I don't know," Chee said. "I don't know why." But he knew there must be a reason. Had to be. If he could just be smart enough to figure it out. And that brought him back to the picture.

"Was the address on that picture . . ." he began, but Margaret Sosi was talking.

"It doesn't matter now," she said. "Whether it was a ghost hogan or not. In just a few hours I'll be cured of that. Mr. Littleben will finish just when the sun comes up. And I feel cured already."

Chee did not feel cured. The ghost sickness clung to him as heavy as a rain-soaked saddle blanket. He felt dizzy with it. Sick.

"The address on that picture," he continued. "Was it the same place you went when you went to Los Angeles?"

"Yes. That's how I knew to go there. I wanted to find the family, and that woman there told me what bus to catch to get to the place of Bentwoman and Bentwoman's Daughter."

"And all it said on the picture was 'Don't trust anybody'?"

" 'Don't trust nobody," Margaret corrected. "That was all, and 'Leroy' down at the bottom."

That was exactly all he had learned. He told Margaret Sosi that when this was over he would drive her back to Santa Fe and pick up the picture card. But even as he said it, his instinct told him that even if he held the card in his hand it would tell him nothing he didn't already know. The final piece of the puzzle found; the puzzle unresolved.

They had eaten then, about thirty altogether, from two pots of mutton stew and a basket of

fry bread. They ate bakery-made oatmeal cook-
ies for dessert, and drank Pepsi-Cola and coffee.
Hosteen Littleben came over and agreed to pu-
rify the Begay Four Mountains Bundle, a rite
that involved rinsing it with some of the emetic
made for the patient to drink when the ceremonial ended.

"Frank Sam, he tells me you're going to be a
yataalii. Said you already know most of the
Blessing Way and you're learning some of the
others. That's a good thing." Hosteen Littleben
was short and fat, and when he walked he tilted
a little because of a stiff leg. His two pigtails
were black, but his mustache was almost gray
and his face was a map of deep-cut lines. If
Frank Sam Nakai was right, if Hosteen Littleben was the youngest medicine man left who
knew the Ghostway, then the People would be
losing another piece of their inheritance from
the Holy People.

"Yes," Chee said. "Learning the songs is a
good thing." Was a good thing, he thought. The
verb is "was."

And then it was time for the final segment of
the Ghostway chant. The very last glow of twilight was gone, the moon climbing, the mesa
dark, and the lights of Albuquerque glowing
against Sandia Mountain forty miles (and a
world) away. Hosteen Littleben would twice

cover the earthen floor of the hogan with the ceremonial's elaborate dry paintings, illustrating episodes in the mythic adventures by which the Holy People resolved the problem caused by death's disruptive residue. Margaret Sosi would sit surrounded by this abstract imagery, and by the love and care of this ragtag remnant of the Turkey Clan, and be returned to beauty and *hozro,* cleansed of the ghost. Chee didn't follow the participants back into the hogan. To do that properly, one's mind must be right—free of wrong thoughts, anger, and disappointment and all things negative. Chee stayed out in the cold, his mind full of wrong thoughts.

Leroy Gorman arrived a little later, parking a white Chevy among the cluster of vehicles in the yard of the Yellow place. Chee watched him walk up the slope to the hogan, the moonlight reflecting from the crown of his Stetson and the blue and white plaid of his mackinaw.

"Hell of a place to find," he said. "The police station was closed, but they had your map pinned there on the door. But even with a map, I've been all over the landscape. Taking the wrong turns. How do they make a living out here?"

"They don't make much of one," Chee said.

Gorman was staring at the hogan, from which the sound of Littleben's chant was issuing again, and then back down the slope at the shabby cluster of shacks and outbuildings that housed the families of the Yellow outfit. He shook his head. "My kinfolks," he said.

"What did you mean when you wrote 'Don't trust nobody' on that picture?"

Gorman was staring at the hogan again. For a moment, the question didn't seem to register. "What?" he said.

"The picture you mailed to Albert, back in Los Angeles. Why did you write that on it?"

"I didn't," Leroy Gorman said. "I don't know what the hell you're talking about."

"You said you'd written to your brother back in L.A. Just good wishes. That sort of stuff. We find this card. It's addressed to Albert, and it says 'Don't trust nobody.'"

"Not me," Leroy Gorman said.

Chee studied him, trying to see his face in the moon shadow under the broad felt brim. He could see only the glint of reflection from the lens of his glasses.

"I wrote right after I got to Shiprock. I sent Albert a letter and I told him I was all right. And I asked him to call somebody for me and tell 'em I'd be away for a while, and not to worry."

"Who?"

Leroy Gorman didn't say anything for a while. Then he shrugged. "Friend of mine. A woman." He shrugged again. "Didn't want her worried and all pissed off. Had her phone number but I wasn't sure of her address, so I sent Al the number and asked him to tell her."

"So how did Albert get this photograph of you standing there by your trailer, with the note on the back?"

"Part of that's easy," Leroy said. "I sent him the photograph. Put it in the letter. But I didn't write nothing on it."

"You mailed him the Polaroid photo then?"

"Yeah. Set the camera over on the hood of my car, and set the timer and stood over by the trailer while it took the picture. But I didn't write on the back of it. I think if you do that it spoils the picture. The ink works through."

Chee digested that. The final piece dropped into the puzzle and created a new puzzle. Who had written *Don't Trust Nobody* on the back of that damned photograph? And when? And how had they gotten it. And why? Why? Why?

"Somebody sent it," Chee said. "In the mail. It had a 'Postage Due' thing stamped on it. And somebody signed it 'Leroy.'"

"Said 'Don't trust anybody'? Nothing else?"

"Right," Chee said.

"Who could it have been?" Gorman asked. He pushed his hat brim back, and the moonlight lit his lined face and reflected from his glasses. "And why?"

Those were exactly the questions in Chee's mind.

They hung in his mind, unanswered. He and Gorman had poked at the questions for a while, adding nothing to their understanding. And Chee had explained to Gorman that it wouldn't be proper for Gorman, a stranger, to enter the hogan at this stage of the ceremony. If he'd arrived an hour earlier, he could have met his niece and his other kinsmen at their supper. Now he would have to wait until dawn, when the ritual ended. Gorman wandered over to the fire, where spectators who weren't joining in the hogan ceremonial were visiting. Chee heard him introducing himself and, a little later, the sound of laughter. Leroy Gorman had found at least the fringes of his family.

Chee went back to his pickup and turned on the engine. No place left to look now. He'd drive Margaret Sosi to Santa Fe, get the picture and look at it, and see what had already been described to him. That would be the end of that. There were no loose ends, nothing. Just a sequence of murderous incidents which seemed to violate reason. They certainly violated Frank Sam Nakai's basic rules for the universe—which had become Jim Chee's rules. Everything is connected. Cause and effect is the universal rule. Nothing happens without motive or without effect. The wing of the corn beetle affects the direction of the wind, the way the sand drifts, the way the light reflects into the eye of man beholding his reality. All is part of totality, and in this totality man finds his *hozro*, his way of walking in harmony, with beauty all around him.

"Don't trust nobody," Chee said aloud. He turned on the heater, confirmed that the engine was still too cold to help, and switched it off again. People were sleeping in the cars and trucks around Yellow's house, and in bedrolls on the ground, waiting for dawn, when Margaret Sosi would emerge from the hogan with the soot washed from her face. She would drink the bitter emetic Hosteen Littleben would have prepared for her, vomit up the last traces of her ghost sickness, and be happily returned to the beauty of her way.

Chee's mind wouldn't leave it alone. Why the warning against trust? he thought. Who wasn't to be trusted? Should he take the advice himself? Just who was he trusting in this affair?

There was Shaw. The cop motivated by love for a friend and desire for justice. Was that credible? Chee thought about Shaw for a while and came up with nothing helpful. There was

Sharkey. Chee could think of no reason not to trust what he'd learned from the FBI agent—which was nothing much. There was even Up-church. Had he done something untrustworthy before he died? Who else was Chee depending on? Leroy Gorman. He'd learned nothing much from Leroy, except for Leroy's denial that he'd written the warning on the picture. Chee con-sidered that a moment. Did he trust Gorman? Of course not, no more than he trusted Albert Gor-man's landlady. He simply trusted them to be-have in the way they were conditioned to behave. Just as you trusted the mailman to de-liver mail. Chee remembered Albert Gorman's mailbox, shielding it with his body so Gorman's landlady couldn't see that he was checking its contents. Abruptly a whole new line of thought opened. The letter Leroy Gorman had mailed would have been delivered to that mailbox, visi-ble to Mrs. Day—the landlady who was being paid to keep McNair informed. But the picture, mailed as a postcard with an address, but no stamp and no return address, would have been delivered just a little differently. The mailman would have tapped at the door and collected the postage due. Mrs. Day would have had no chance to intercept that. Was that important? Chee could see how it might be. He considered.

"Ah," he said. If he was thinking correctly, the

McNair people would have known Leroy Gorman was hidden at Shiprock very soon after he got there. Mrs. Day would have seen the letter Leroy Gorman had mailed in Albert's mailbox, and noted the return address, and made her $100 call. And in such a small community they could have found a stranger. Not quickly, perhaps, because Albert obviously had the photograph and they didn't. But they could have found him. Apparently they didn't try. Why not?

Chee sighed. What about the card? Leroy Gorman said he'd mailed the Polaroid photograph in an envelope and hadn't written the warning on it. But the photograph had "Postage Due" stamped on it, and an address. What explained that? Two photographs? Hardly possible with a Polaroid print. Albert Gorman had told old man Berger he received the photograph from his brother, that he was worried. The "Wish you were here" note Leroy said he'd written would hardly provoke worry. The "Don't trust nobody" message would.

Chee closed his eyes, shutting out the moonlight and the sound of Mr. Littleben's chanting as best he could to better reproduce the scene on the Silver Threads lawn. There was Mr. Berger, using his hands to tell the story of the blond man coming, of Albert Gorman slamming the door on the blond man's hand. Gorman had told Berger that he wasn't supposed to go to Shiprock, but he was going anyway. Berger believed the blond man had come to prevent that. That hadn't made sense to Chee then, and it made no sense now. If they hadn't found Leroy, they would have wanted Al to go find him for them. What if they had found him. Would it matter then? Perhaps.

Abruptly Chee sat bolt upright, eyes open. It would matter a lot if the man Albert Gorman found when he found the trailer was not his brother. What if the McNair people had found Leroy in his trailer, and removed him, and replaced him? But that couldn't possibly work. Chee did a quick scan of his memory for reasons it couldn't work.

There were none. Upchurch, who would have recognized the switch instantly, was dead. Farmer, the only man in the U.S.D.A.'s office Upchurch had trusted with his witnesses, was far away working for a private law firm in San Francisco. Who did that leave who would know Leroy Gorman? Sharkey? Not likely. Sharkey would know he had one under his wing, would be in telephone contact, would be alert. But he would also stay away to avoid drawing any attention to the man.

Looking back on it, Chee could never say exactly when enlightenment came. First he finally really understood how the postcard had originated. Leroy Gorman must have realized he had been found. They must have sent Vaggan to dispose of him. Perhaps he'd seen Vaggan first. He would have known instantly that the Witness Protection Program had failed. He had been trying to talk his brother into cooperating with the Feds. Now he knew that was a fatal mistake. He'd be desperate to warn his brother. He'd managed to jot the address and the warning on the only thing he had with him that would drop through a mailbox slot—the Polaroid print. "Don't trust nobody" included the FBI, the McNair bunch, and everyone else.

After that breakthrough, the rest of it became clear and simple. The death of Upchurch must have triggered it, and it didn't matter whether Shaw was right, or the coroner. Probably the death had been natural. What mattered was that McNair knew of it quickly, and recognized the chance it offered. Upchurch's secrecy had been the downfall of Clan McNair, but now it presented McNair a way out, a witness switch. It made what had happened at the Begay hogan totally logical. Everything had to be done to avoid raising any question, drawing any attention to the man in the aluminum trailer at Shiprock. Once again Frank Sam Nakai's immutable law of cause and motivation was confirmed.

About then, Jim Chee began thinking of who the man he'd been calling Leroy Gorman might really be, and the implication of what this man was doing. And he realized that if things went as planned he might not leave Mesa Gigante alive. And neither would Margaret Billy Sosi.

> 26 <

CHEE UNLOCKED THE GLOVE BOX, fumbled among the maps, tools, and papers in it, and pulled out his pistol. It was a short-barreled .38 caliber revolver, and Chee looked at it without pleasure. Nothing against this particular pistol; it was just that Chee had no fondness for any of them and wasn't particularly good at using them. Keeping up his marksmanship certification, a condition of employment, was an annual chore. While he always managed to pass, there was never any margin to spare. Now, however, the heft of the pistol was reassuring in his hand. He examined it, made sure it was loaded, and cocked and uncocked it. Then he dropped it into the side pocket of his coat. That out of the way, it was time to make a plan. That involved trying to figure out what was likely to happen here.

The key to it all was simple: Leroy Gorman was not Leroy Gorman. He might be Beno, or whatever his name was—the Navajo Shaw said the grand jury had indicted and who had never been picked up. That made sense. Shaw had said finding him was tough because he had no arrest record, which meant no pictures or fingerprints, and no useful information. Thus nobody was going to recognize him. And when the time came for McNair to go to trial, a Navajo identified as Leroy Gorman would be placed on the witness stand, and how would they work it then? Chee guessed he knew. When the D.A. examined him, he'd recite his testimony in a halting, uncertain way, raising doubt in the jury. Then, under cross examination, he'd say that he'd been coached in what to say by Upchurch; that Upchurch had given him all this information, and assured him it was true, and warned him that if he didn't recite in court he'd be sent to prison as a thief. He would say that he actually knew none of it; he was simply passing along what the FBI agent had told him. And that, of course, would taint everything any other prosecution witness said, and raise at least a reasonable doubt, and McNair would go home free.

The genuine Leroy Gorman was undoubtedly dead. Carefully dead. They would never want his body found.

Chee reconsidered. Sharkey? No problem.

Leroy's warning had been mailed almost immediately after he was put in place. There was almost no chance that Sharkey would have seen him. So Leroy Gorman was not Gorman. Chee found himself thinking of the man as Grayson once again. What to do about Grayson?

Chee climbed out of his pickup and looked toward the hogan. The chanting of Littleben was silent now. Chee imagined him on his knees, building the final sand painting. With the exception of two men and a very fat woman talking beside the fire, those waiting for dawn to bring the ceremony's end were waiting in the relative warmth of their cars. Chee stared at Gorman's Chevy, trying to see if the man was in it. He couldn't tell. He put his hand on the pistol in his coat pocket, took two steps toward Gorman's car. Then he stopped. The entire theory suddenly was nonsense—the product of being hit on the head and too many hours without sleep. He imagined himself arresting Gorman.

"What's the charge?"

"I think you're impersonating a federal witness."

"That's a crime?"

"Well, it might be."

And he imagined himself standing in front of Largo's desk, Largo looking at him, wordless, sad, stricken with the latest Chee stupidity. And

Sharkey, maybe, at the back of the room, too furious to be coherent.

Chee walked back to his pickup truck and leaned against it, trying to think. If Gorman was a plant working for McNair, what would he have done when Chee called him and told him the Sosi girl was found, and invited him to come and meet her? He wouldn't have come. Of course not, because Margaret Sosi would have seen Leroy Gorman's picture and would recognize he wasn't Leroy Gorman, and that would screw everything up. He came, so of course he was the genuine Leroy Gorman.

Chee thought some more. His theory, wrong as it was, made everything click into place. Everything. It explained what had happened at the Begay hogan. Nothing else explained that. So the man was an imposter and he'd come anyway.

But of course! Grayson had to come. Here Chee would meet Sosi, see the photograph, know Grayson wasn't Leroy Gorman, and everything would collapse around him. So he'd come, late enough so that Margaret Sosi wouldn't see him in any decent light. And so far, for that matter, she hadn't seen him at all. He'd come because it was a last chance to get the picture back before it did any serious harm, and to eliminate Sosi, who'd seen the picture.

Chee had a second chilling thought. Whoever he was, he wouldn't have come alone if he could help it. He would have called Los Angeles and had Vaggan sent to help. How long would that take? A chartered plane, a rented car. Chee tried to calculate. Plenty of time to fly to Albuquerque and then drive. An even worse thought occurred to him. Vaggan hadn't waited around Los Angeles all the time Chee was mending in the hospital there. More likely he'd have confirmed, somehow, that the Sosi girl had left and he had driven directly to the reservation to look for her. That would have made getting here simple indeed. He might have driven out with Gorman. Chee doubted that. He'd have brought his own vehicle. And where would he have left it?

Chee had a possible answer for that. He trotted down Mr. Yellow's entrance track to the road that had brought him up Mesa Gigante. And then he walked, keeping well away from it. The ruined hogan the girl in the police station had described to him was about a mile away, near the rim of the mesa. Chee approached it cautiously, keeping behind the cover of junipers when he could, keeping low when there was no cover. Where the track forked off from the road toward the ruin, Chee stopped, knelt, and studied the ground. Tire tracks. The moonlight was dim now, slanting from near the western horizon, but the tracks were plain enough. Made today. Made only hours ago, with neither wind nor time to soften them. Still on his knees, Chee started toward the hogan, out of sight just over a fold of land. No Cañoncito Navajo would drive in there at night and brave a ghost. The hogan had been marked on the map he'd left for the man who wasn't Leroy Gorman. The man must have left the map for Vaggan, and Vaggan—obviously, from what had happened at the Begay place—had taken the trouble to educate himself about Navajo attitudes about ghosts and ghost hogans.

Chee moved cautiously down the track, keeping behind the junipers. He didn't have to go far. After less than fifty yards he had enough visibility over the hillock to see the top of what remained of the hogan's wall. And over the wall, the top of a dark van. Chee stared at it, remembering the last time he had seen it—and what he had seen in the frantic moment he had been inside it, remembering the locked gun rack behind the driver's seat and what it had held. He'd seen an automatic shotgun, something that had looked like an M16 automatic rifle, and at least two smaller automatic weapons—an arsenal.

It occurred to Chee, fairly early in his walk back to the Yellow place, that if things went bad here—as they seemed likely to—it was purely because of Jim Chee's stupidity. He had found Margaret Sosi for them, and then he had called them down on her. Two other things also seemed apparent. Vaggan would do nothing overt here, at this sing, because he was smart enough to know how long it would take him to drive from here to anyplace he could lose himself. Empty, roadless country made troubles for law enforcement, but it also had advantages, and one of them was that roadblocks are extremely efficient. If you have a wheeled vehicle, there's no place to go with it. If you don't, hiding is easy enough, but there's no water. So Vaggan would wait. Follow them away from here, probably. Pass them on the highway, perhaps, and finish it all with a burst of fire from that automatic rifle. Or at least follow Margaret Sosi. Chee, until he saw the photograph, would be harmless. And he'd told the substitute Gorman that the picture was in Santa Fe.

Finally it occurred to him that he had one advantage. He knew Grayson was the enemy. He knew Vaggan was out there waiting. What he didn't know, not yet, was how to use that advantage. He moved rapidly through the snakeweed and cactus, back toward Yellow's hogan. On the eastern horizon now he could make out the ragged outline of the Sandias and the Manzano Mountains, back-lighted by the first glimmer of dawn. He had very little time to decide.

The fire had been rebuilt with a fresh supply of logs and was sending sparks high above the hogan when Chee returned. Everybody was up, waiting for the final act of the drama that would free Margaret Sosi from the ghost that rode her and return her to the ways of beauty. Chee searched through the crowd, looking for Grayson. He spotted him at the edge of the cluster just as the sound of Littleben's chanting stopped. It was a moment too early. Chee ducked back into the crowd, away from Grayson's vision.

The door of the hogan opened out, and Littleben emerged, trailed by Margaret Sosi. He held a small clay pot in his right hand and a pair of prayer sticks, elaborately painted and feathered, in the other. He held the feathered *pahos* high, their shafts crossed in an X. *"Now our daughter will drink this brew,"* he chanted.

"Now our daughter, she being daughter of Black God,
Now our daughter, she being daughter of Talking God,
Now our daughter, she being Blue Flint Girl,

Now our daughter, she being White Shell
Girl,
Now our daughter will drink away the evil,
Now our daughter will return to hozro,
Now our daughter will walk again in the
male rain falling,
Now our daughter will walk with the dark
mist around her,
Now our daughter will go with beauty above
her.
Now our daughter . . ."

Chee had lost sight of Grayson again. He
turned away from the poetry of the chant to
look for him. When the time was right, he
wanted to know exactly where he could find the
man. He wanted Grayson close. And Grayson
was close. He had simply moved a little nearer
the hogan. But he was still keeping himself
where Margaret Sosi couldn't see him—or so it
seemed to Chee. It also seemed to Chee that
Margaret Sosi would hardly notice him. She
had drunk the steaming emetic now and was
staring at the east. She was supposed to vomit
just as the red first rim of the sun was visible on
the horizon. It was apparent from the strained
look on her face that her inclination was to
vomit instantly. But there, suddenly, was the

rim of the sun. It was time to use his one advantage.

Chee hurried through the onlookers to Grayson and grabbed him by the elbow.

"Leroy," he said. "Trouble."

"What?" Grayson looked startled.

"Vaggan is here," Chee said. "Big blond man who's a killer for McNair. He's got his van parked out there."

"Vaggan?" Grayson said. "My God."

"He must be waiting until this is over. Until the crowd breaks up. Or he's waiting for you to leave and he'll follow you."

"Yeah," Grayson said. He looked suitably nervous.

"There's another way out of here," Chee said. "On past this place, the road winds down the other side of the mesa. It's bad but it's passable."

Around them the spectators were laughing and clapping. Margaret Sosi had gotten rid of her evil and was returned to *hozro*. Her relatives crowded around her.

"Just turn left where Yellow's drive comes off the road and keep driving. I'll get Margaret and follow you."

"Left," Grayson said. "Okay."

He ran for his car. Chee hurried through the crowd to Margaret Sosi. She was talking to an old woman, with Littleben standing beside her.

"Come on," Chee said. "Vaggan is here. We've got to run."

Margaret Sosi looked puzzled. With the ghost blacking washed away, she also looked pale. "Vaggan?"

"The big man back in L.A. Remember? The one who pretended to be a cop. The one who hit me."

"Oh," Margaret Sosi said. She hurried along with him. "Good-by. Good-by. And thank you."

Grayson's Chevy was roaring down the track away from the Yellow place. Chee started his pickup, backed it around in a flurry of dust, and roared down the track. At the bottom of the arroyo, he slid the pickup to a stop, shifted into low gear, and edged it carefully up the wash, banging and slamming over the rocks and scraping through the thickets of mountain mahogany and chamiza that flourished in the stream bottom. When he was far enough from the track to be out of sight he turned off the engine. Margaret Sosi was looking at him, the question on her face.

He had time enough to explain it all to her, because now there was nothing to do but wait. . . .

"And so," Chee concluded, "I told the guy who's pretending to be Gorman that I'd spotted Vaggan, and I told him to make a run for it on a road down the other side of the mesa, and I told him you and I would follow. He drove right off, but where he'll go is to tell Vaggan we've seen him, and that we're running."

"But when he goes after us—" Margaret Sosi began.

"We give him time to do that, and then we run ourselves."

"But why didn't we just go down the other side?"

"The road doesn't go anywhere. That's what they told me at the police station. It wanders around a little up here and turns into wagon tracks. But there's no other way down off the mesa; just back the way we came. The only way down is right past where Vaggan is parked."

"Oh," Margaret Sosi said. "Okay."

They sat in silence.

"How long do we wait?"

Exactly the question in Chee's mind. Chee had counted four of the seven vehicles that had been parked at the Yellow place passing on the track behind them. Now track and road were silent. The other three, he guessed, must be staying for breakfast and a visit. He had to allow enough time for Grayson to reach the old hogan, and give Vaggan the word, and for them to drive back past Yellow's turnoff. More than that was time wasted—because it probably would not take Vaggan long to realize the road was playing out into nothing. But less than that would be fatal. Chee had no illusions about the outcome of any shooting match between his pistol and Vaggan's automatic weapon.

He squeezed his eyes shut, trying to estimate time elapsed and match it with Vaggan's actions.

"About now, I think." He started the engine again and bumped the pickup backward down the arroyo floor. At the intersection, nothing was in sight on the road in either direction. He had allowed a little more time than necessary, which meant pursuit would be a little quicker than it might have been. He roared down the rutted dirt. Dawn was bright enough now to make headlights needless, but still dim enough to make it hard to see the uneven road surface. He skidded the pickup around the sharp turn where the road dipped suddenly over the mesa rim, braked again where it made another hairpin bend around a great upthrust of sand-stone and slate, then jerked the wheel sharply to the right to bend it around the wall of stone.

Just behind the wall, the big brown van was parked, blocking the way. Vaggan was standing behind it, the automatic rifle aimed at Chee's windshield. Chee stood on the brakes, sending the truck into a sidewise skid that stopped it parallel to the van. He shifted frantically into reverse, spinning the rear wheels in the road-side sand. Grayson was standing beside the road, not fifteen feet away, a pistol pointed at Chee.

"Kill the engine," Vaggan shouted. "Or I kill you now."

Chee killed the engine.

"Stick your hands out the window where I can see them," Vaggan ordered.

Chee put his hands out the window.

"Now reach down, outside the door where I can see the hand, and open the door, and get out, and keep your hands where I can see them. Your hand gets out of my sight and I kill you right then."

Chee opened the door and stepped out on the ground. He was conscious of the weight of the .38 in the right-hand pocket of his coat. How long would it take him to reach it and shoot Vaggan? Far, far, far too long.

"I'm going to handcuff you and put you in the van here with me," Vaggan said. He was walking toward Chee, the automatic rifle aimed at Chee's midsection. "And then you and the girl and all of us will go someplace where it's quieter and we can talk this all over. Where's your pistol?"

"No pistol," Chee said. "I'm off duty. It's back at my place in Shiprock."

"I'm not stupid," Vaggan said. "If I was stupid I'd be off chasing down that road where you told Beno you'd be. Lay down on your face. On the ground. Hands and feet spread. Beno, come here and get his gun. Probably a shoulder holster or under his belt."

Chee stood, trying to think of something useful.

"Down," Vaggan said. He speared Chee in the chest with the rifle barrel.

Chee dropped to his knees gasping. He knew exactly what was coming. Vaggan would take them to some more isolated spot, where the gunshots would not bring someone immediately to check. Then he would kill them. Just two shots, Chee guessed. One each. The less shots, the less chance of arousing curiosity.

"Down," Vaggan ordered, jabbing Chee in the back with the rifle. Chee dropped to his belly.

"There it is," Vaggan said. "In his coat pock- . . ."

The sound of the gunshot drowned out the rest of it. Vaggan had shot him, but he felt nothing except the pain where Vaggan's rifle barrel had stuck him. For a crazy split second Chee's mind searched for the point of impact, for the feeling that the bullet must be causing. He saw, past the clump of snakeweed in which his cheek was pressed, the motion of Vaggan falling, falling sideways, arms thrown out.

"Don't," someone screamed. "Don't."

In another fragment of that moment, Chee realized he had not been shot. The voice was Grayson's, and as he scrambled up from the dirt, his mind was making the automatic correction from Grayson to Beno. He staggered to his feet, trying to tear the pistol out of his coat pocket, trying to cock it. But he didn't need the pistol.

Margaret Sosi was leaning out of the driver's side of the pickup, a huge revolver gripped in both hands. The revolver was aimed at Beno. Vaggan was sprawled on his side, face turned toward the earth, one leg slowly bending toward his chest, his rifle in the dirt beside him.

"Don't," Beno screamed again. "Don't shoot." Beno held his arms stretched high over his head.

Chee finally got his own pistol untangled from the jacket pocket. Beno had no weapon now. He'd dropped his pistol beside Vaggan's leg. Chee picked it up. He heard a metallic rapping sound. Margaret Sosi was shaking, the barrel of her pistol rattling against the metal of the pickup window. Where had she gotten the gun? And then he remembered. It must be the same pistol Vaggan had dropped when Chee had hit him with the flashlight back in Los Angeles. She'd kept it. That was the sensible sort of thing Margaret Billy Sosi could be expected to do. And she had shot Vaggan with his own gun.

> **27** <

WHEN CHEE GOT BACK TO SHIPROCK, the letter was in his mailbox. He saw immediately that the handwriting on the envelope was Mary Landon's and that it was thick enough to contain two or three sheets of paper. A long letter. He put it in his jacket pocket along with what seemed to be a solicitation from an insurance company.

Back in his trailer, he put the letter on the table. He hung up his jacket and his hat, locked his pistol in the drawer, and poured a pot of water into his Mr. Coffee machine. He stripped and took a hot shower. That left him feeling clean and a little more relaxed. But he was tired. Absolutely, utterly tired, and it was that, probably, that was causing his head to ache. He sat beside the table in his bathrobe and looked at the letter. In a moment, he would open it. Was there anything else he needed to do first—any

loose ends? He could think of none. The heli-
copter ambulance had come from the University of New Mexico Medical Center and its
attendants had inspected Vaggan, their faces
grim. And then they had flown away with him.
The New Mexico State Policemen had come to
the Cañoncito Police Station with two FBI
agents Chee had never met. They had taken
Beno off Chee's hands. Margaret Sosi had eaten
breakfast with him in the Albuquerque bus station, and had made a telephone call, and had
shortly thereafter been picked up by a middle-
aged woman who Chee gathered was the
mother of a schoolmate from Isleta Pueblo. The
woman had not seemed to approve of Chee and
had fussed over Margaret and taken her away to
get some sleep. And then he'd checked into a
motel intending to sleep a little himself. But he
was too tense to sleep. So he'd made the 200-
mile drive back to Shiprock, and called Captain
Largo to tell him what had happened, and
picked up his mail and come home.

No loose ends. Nothing. All finished. He
pushed the envelope with his finger, turning it
around so that he could read his name, right
side up, in Mary Landon's bold, reckless handwriting.

Then he opened it.

My darling Jim,

Why am I writing you a letter? Because I want to make sure I manage to say just what I want to say so that you understand it. Maybe that will help me understand it, too.

What I have to say is that I have a friend named Theresa McGill who when she was in college fell in love with a man who was just finishing with the seminary—learning to be a Catholic priest. She loved him, maybe not as much as I love you, but she loved him a lot. And they got married, which meant, of course, he didn't go through with being ordained a priest. He got a job teaching, and they had a daughter, and I thought for a long time that she was happy. But last summer she told me how it really was. She'd notice him being very quiet. Maybe just looking out the window or sitting out in the backyard alone. Or taking long walks by himself. And one Saturday afternoon she followed him, and she saw him go into a church. An empty church. No services. No one there. But he stayed inside for an hour. Theresa told me that she has been living with that. She loves her husband, and she knows she deprived

him of something that was terribly important to him. And always will be important.

Well, that's what I'm trying to say. I don't
want that to happen to us, so I want to tell
you that I've changed my mind. I won't
marry you on my terms—that we get off the
reservation and raise our family somewhere else. Maybe I will marry you on your
terms—that we live here among your people. If you still want to. But I've got to have
time to think about it. So I'm going home—
back to Wisconsin. I'm going to talk to my
family, and walk around in the snow, and
go ice skating, and see what happens to my
mind. But I'm not going to change my mind
about one thing—I'm not going to force my
Jim Chee to be a white man. . . .

Chee put the letter on the tabletop beside the
envelope and tried to examine himself for a reaction. He was tired, and suddenly sleepy as
well. He was not surprised, particularly. This
letter was exactly in character for Mary. Exactly. He should have known it. Perhaps he did.
Otherwise, why the lack of surprise? And what
else did he feel? A sort of blank numbness, as if
all this concerned someone else. That was fatigue too, he guessed. Tomorrow the numbness
would be gone. And tomorrow he'd decide what

to do. Call Mary, probably. But what would he say to her? He couldn't seem to think what it would be. He found himself thinking, instead, of Leo Littleben, Junior, and wondering if Littleben really was going to be the last man alive to know the Ghostway ceremony.

He got up, already stiff, poured himself a cup of coffee, and leaned against the sink while he sipped it. When he finished it, he would go to bed and sleep until spring. And when he awoke, whenever that was, he would think about Mary Landon's letter and what he should do about it. He would also get in touch with Frank Sam Nakai and ask his uncle to arrange for Hosteen Littleben to sing a Ghostway cure for him. And then, he thought, he would talk to Littleben. Feel him out about what he would charge Chee to teach him the ritual. It would be a good thing for a younger man to know it.

And thinking that, Chee fell across his bed with his bathrobe still on and went, almost instantly, to sleep.

Here's Chapter One from Tony Hillerman's
Coyote Waits,
on sale now from HarperPaperbacks.

> **1** <

OFFICER JIM CHEE was thinking that either his right front tire was a little low or there was something wrong with the shock on that side. On the other hand, maybe the road grader operator hadn't been watching the adjustment on his blade and he'd tilted the road. Whatever the cause, Chee's patrol car was pulling just a little to the right. He made the required correction, frowning. He was dog-tired.

The radio speaker made an uncertain noise, then produced the voice of Officer Delbert Nez. ". . . running on fumes. I'm going to have to buy some of that high-cost Red Rock gasoline or walk home."

"If you do, I advise paying for it out of your pocket," Chee said. "Better than explaining to the captain why you forgot to fill it up."

"I think . . ." Nez said and then the voice faded out.

"Your signal's breaking up," Chee said. "I don't read you." Nez was using Unit 44, a notorious gas hog. Something wrong with the fuel pump, maybe. It was always in the shop and nobody ever quite fixed it.

Silence. Static. Silence. The steering seemed to be better now. Probably not a low tire. Probably . . . And then the radio intruded again.

". . . catch the son-of-a-bitch with the smoking paint gun in his hand," Nez was saying. "I'll bet then . . ." The Nez voice vanished, replaced by silence.

"I'm not reading you," Chee said into his mike. "You're breaking up."

Which wasn't unusual. There were a dozen places on the twenty-five thousand square miles the Navajos called the Big Rez where radio transmission was blocked for a variety of reasons. Here between the monolithic volcanic towers of Ship Rock, the Carrizo Range, and the Chuska Mountains was just one of them. Chee presumed these radio blind spots were caused by the mountains but there were other theories. Deputy Sheriff Cowboy Dashee insisted that it had something to do with magnetism in the old volcanic necks that stuck up here and there, like great black cathedrals. Old Thomasina Bigthumb had told him once that she thought witches caused the problem. True, this part of the Reservation was notorious for witches, but it was also true that Old Lady Bigthumb blamed witches for just about everything.

Then Chee heard Delbert Nez again. The voice was very faint at first. ". . . his car," Delbert was saying. (Or was it ". . . his truck"? Or ". . . his pickup"? Exactly, precisely, what had Delbert Nez said?) Suddenly the transmission became clearer, the sound of Delbert's delighted laughter. "I'm gonna get him this time," Delbert Nez said.

Chee picked up the mike. "Who are you getting?" he said. "Do you need assistance?"

"My phantom painter," Nez seemed to say. At least it sounded like that. The reception was going sour again, fading, breaking up into static.

"Can't read you," Chee said. "You need assistance?"

Through the fade-out, through the static, Nez seemed to say "No." Again, laughter.

"I'll see you at Red Rock then," Chee said. "It's your turn to buy."

There was no response to that at all, except static, and none was needed. Nez worked up U.S. 666 out of the Navajo Tribal Police headquarters at Window Rock, covering from Yah-Ta-Hey northward. Chee patrolled down 666 from the Shiprock subagency police station, and when they met they had coffee and talked. Having it this evening at the service station-post office-grocery store at Red Rock had been decided earlier, and it was upon Red Rock that they were converging. Chee was driving down the dirt road that wandered back and forth across the Arizona–New Mexico border southward from Biklabito. Nez was driving westward from 666 on the asphalt of Navajo Route 33. Nez, having pavement, would have been maybe fifteen minutes early. But now he seemed to have an arrest to make. That would even things up.

There was lightning in the cloud over the Chuskas now, and Chee's patrol car had stopped pulling to the right and was pulling to the left. Probably not a tire, he thought. Probably the road grader operator had noticed his maladjusted blade and overcorrected. At least it wasn't the usual washboard effect that pounded your kidneys.

It was twilight—twilight induced early by the impending thunderstorm—when Chee pulled his patrol car off the dirt and onto the pavement of Route 33. No sign of Nez. In fact, no sign of any headlights, just the remains of what had been a blazing red sunset. Chee pulled past the gasoline pumps at the Red Rock station and parked behind the trading post. No Unit 44 police car where Nez usually parked it. He inspected his front tires, which seemed fine. Then he looked around. Three pickups and a blue Chevy sedan. The sedan belonged to the new evening clerk at the trading post. Good-looking girl, but he couldn't come up with her name. Where was Nez? Maybe he actually had caught his paint-spraying vandal. Maybe the fuel pump on old 44 had died.

No Nez inside either. Chee nodded to the girl reading behind the cash register. She rewarded him with a shy smile. What was her name? Sheila? Suzy? Something like that. She was a Towering House Dineh, and therefore in no way linked to Chee's own Slow Talking Clan. Chee remembered that. It was the automatic checkoff any single young Navajo conducts—male or female—making sure the one who attracted you wasn't a sister, or cousin, or niece in the tribe's complex clan system, and thereby rendered taboo by incest rules.

The glass coffee-maker pot was two-thirds full, usually a good sign, and it smelled fresh. He picked up a fifty-cent-size Styrofoam cup, poured it full, and sipped. Good, he thought. He picked out a package containing two chocolate-frosted Twinkies. They'd go well with the coffee.

Back at the cash register, he handed the Towering House girl a five-dollar bill.

"Has Delbert Nez been in? You remember him? Sort of stocky, little mustache. Really ugly policeman."

"I thought he was cute," the Towering House girl said, smiling at Chee.

"Maybe you just like policemen?" Chee said. What the devil was her name?

"Not all of them," she said. "It depends."

"On whether they've arrested your boyfriend," Chee said. She wasn't married. He remembered Delbert had told him that. ("Why don't you find out these things for yourself," Delbert had said. "Before I got married, I would have known essential information like that. Wouldn't have had to ask. My wife finds out I'm making clan checks on the chicks, I'm in deep trouble.")

"I don't have a boyfriend," the Towering House girl said. "Not right now. And, no. Delbert hasn't been in this evening." She handed Chee his change, and giggled. "Has Delbert ever caught his rock painter?"

Chee was thinking maybe he was a little past dealing with girls who giggled. But she had large brown eyes, and long lashes, and perfect skin. Certainly, she knew how to flirt. "Maybe he's catching him right now," he said. "He said something on the radio about it." He noticed she had miscounted his change by a dime, which sort of went with the giggling. "Too much money," Chee said, handing her the dime. "You have any idea who'd be doing that painting?" And then he remembered her name. It was Shirley. Shirley Thompson.

Shirley shuddered, very prettily. "Somebody crazy," she said.

That was Chee's theory too. But he said: "Why crazy?"

"Well, just because," Shirley said, looking serious for the first time. "You know. Who else would do all that work painting that mountain white?"

It wasn't really a mountain. Technically it was probably a volcanic throat—another of those ragged upthrusts of black basalt that jutted out of the prairie here and there east of the Chuskas.

"Maybe he's trying to paint something pretty," Chee said. "Have you ever gone in there and taken a close look at it?"

Shirley shivered. "I wouldn't go there," she said.

"Why not?" Chee asked, knowing why. It probably had some local legend attached to it. Something scary. Probably somebody had been killed there and left his *chindi* behind to haunt the place. And it was tainted by witchcraft gossip. Delbert had been raised back in the Chuska high country west of here and he'd said something about that outcrop—or maybe one nearby—being one of the places where members of the Skinwalker clan were supposed to meet. It was a place to be avoided—and that was part of what had fascinated Officer Delbert Nez with its vandalism.

"It's not just that it's such a totally zany thing to do," Delbert had said. "Putting paint on the side of a rocky ridge, like that. There's a weirdness to it, too. It's a scary place. I don't care what you think about witches, nobody goes there. You do, somebody sees you, and they think you're a skinwalker yourself. I think whoever's doing it must have a purpose. Something specific. I'd like to know who the hell it is. And why."

That had been good enough for Chee, who enjoyed his own little obsessions. He glanced at his watch. Where was Delbert now?

The door opened and admitted a middle-aged woman with her hair tied in a blue cloth. She paid for gasoline, complained about the price, and engaged Shirley in conversation about a sing-dance somebody was planning at the Newcomb school. Chee had another cup of coffee. Two teenaged boys came in, followed by an old man wearing a T-shirt with DON'T WORRY, BE HAPPY printed across the chest. Another woman

came, about Shirley's age, and the sound of
thunder came through the door with her. The
girls chatted and giggled. Chee looked at his
watch again. Delbert was taking too damned
long.

Chee walked out into the night.

The breeze smelled of rain. Chee hurried
around the corner into the total darkness behind the trading post. In the car, he switched on
the radio and tried to raise Nez. Nothing. He
started the engine, and spun the rear wheels in
an impatient start that was totally out of character for him. So was this sudden sense of anxiety.
He switched on his siren and the emergency
flashers.

Chee was only minutes away from the trading
post when he saw the headlights approaching
on Route 33. He slowed, feeling relief. But
before they reached him, he saw the car's right
turn indicator blinking. The vehicle turned
northward, up ahead of him, not Nez's Navajo
Tribal Police patrol car but a battered white
Jeepster. Chee recognized it. It was the car of
the Vietnamese (or Cambodian, or whatever he
was) who taught at the high school in Shiprock.
Chee's headlights briefly lit the driver's face.

The rain started then, a flurry of big, widely
spaced drops splashing the windshield, then a
downpour. Route 33 was wide and smooth,

with a freshly painted centerline to follow. But the rain was more than Chee's wipers could handle. He slowed, listening to the water pound against the roof. Normally rain provoked jubilation in Chee—a feeling natural and primal, bred into dry-country people. Now this joy was blocked by worry and a little guilt. Something had delayed Nez. He should have gone looking for him when the radio blacked out. But it was probably nothing much. Car trouble. An ankle sprained chasing his painter in the dark. Nothing serious.

Lightning illuminated the highway ahead of him, showing it glistening with water and absolutely empty. The flash lit the ragged basalt shape of the formation across the prairie to the south—the outcrop on which Nez's vandal had been splashing his paint. Then the boom of thunder came. The rain slackened, flurried again, slackened again as the squall line of the storm passed. Off to the right Chee saw a glow of light. He stared. It came from down a dirt road that wandered from 33 southward over a ridge, leading eventually to the "outfit" of Old Lady Gorman. Chee let the breath whistle through his teeth. Relief. That would probably be Nez. Guilt fell away from him.

At the intersection, he slowed and stared

down the dirt road. Headlights should be yellow. This light was red. It flickered. Fire.

"Oh, God!" Chee said aloud. A prayer. He geared the patrol car down into second and went slipping and sliding down the muddy track.